Beverly Hills Tutor

By
Libby Keatinge

©Elizabeth Anne Keatinge 2003

PUBLISHED BY ONE HOUR ENTERTAINMENT
LOS ANGELES

Written by: Libby Keatinge
Edited by: Maggie Lohnes, Elizabeth Fore Keatinge
Published by: One Hour Entertainment, LLC
Distributed by Publishers Group West

Special thanks to those who helped make this book possible
especially Heidi Fleiss, Amy Mitoyan, Elissa Guzzardo,
Publishers Group West, Henry Saine, Nikki Ziering,
Colonel Limor and family, Jeff Greene, my wonderful family especially Dr. Dan and Elizabeth Keatinge, Robert, Joe,
Mike and Maggie Lohnes and all others who were supportive, loyal, and kind.

ISBN# 0972016430
First printing in the USA
©2004 One Hour Entertainment

For Papa

"Pretty much all the honest truth-telling there
is in the world is done by children"
-Oliver Wendell Holmes

End Note

*A*va couldn't sleep that night. She had never realized that having more money than she knew what to do with would cause her such distress. She knew it was hers, but was scared that somehow it would be snatched from out of her bank account in the night. She wanted to go to the bank right then and there, take it out and sleep with it, just so she was sure it would be there. Ava went back and forth between feeling excited and feeling nervous. Now she could buy her brother a car-no problem-or anything she had ever wanted for that matter. Her monthly bills now seemed like pennies, where before, she struggled to pay them every month. She saw the numbers over and over in her head...one million dollars, in cash, all her own, and she was still in college. All the questions she had been obsessing about now seemed meaningless. Where will I live when I graduate? What will I do with the rest of my life? Now there was no pressure. Ava could do whatever she wanted.

1

*A*va Fleet had decided she would apply in person. The ad said that resumes were accepted by fax, email, mail, or in person, Monday and Thursday from 12:00-3:00. That morning, she had chosen a seat in the back of her Statistics lecture, and left promptly at the end so she could walk in the light morning drizzle directly to this office on Westwood Boulevard. She was waiting at the door when a tall man in a gray suit opened it at noon.

Ava had always been very prompt, and some times embarrassingly early. Differently from her sorority sisters, she was always actually ready at 8:00 to go out, when her friends always ran the fashionably 20-30 minutes late. She clearly was a book who could not be judged by her cover. Her long blonde hair was tied up in a bun today and her curvy body was strategically concealed by a cream turtleneck and loose fitting black pants. Her babyish face could pass for 16, while her womanly body could have belonged to a woman of 30. She wore only a spot of makeup; some mascara and lip gloss. Her baby face just didn't look right caked with thick makeup.

The waiting room was large, modern, and gray, with a view of Westwood Village. Ava clutched her resume with her French-manicured hands, and felt a pang of nervousness shoot through her body. Educational Advantage was the most prestigious tutoring agency in town. The list of families who used this agency read like the A-list at an Oscar party. If Ava could get a job here, she would easily be able to pay for her textbooks, sorority dues, and even have a little money left over to save. Educational Advantage charged the highest rates because they were the most exclusive.

The other applicants looked quizzically at Ava, as she clearly did not belong in this picture. A young Asian man in his mid twenties held a paper-clipped and dog-eared neatly-organized stack of papers, in a manila folder with a typed "Job" label affixed perfectly on the tab. Amid glances up at the clock, he flipped through his physics book, looked to the right, and mumbled something. Ava thought he must have been quizzing himself. Across the room, a petite dark haired chemistry major fiddled with her bifocals and straightened her pleated skirt every five minutes.

Ava wrote her name neatly on the sign-in sheet and chose a seat in a chair against the wall. She had been waiting 15 minutes when a short man in a black suit opened the door and called out her name. She walked up and cheerily handed him her resume.

He took her resume, skimmed over it, and in a stern monotone voice said, "Good afternoon, Miss Fleet. Thanks for coming by." She followed him down a long hallway lined with expensive plein-air paintings: beautiful landscapes and mountain ranges. He led her into a room with a large oak conference table right in the middle.

He handed her a clipboard stacked with nearly 15 pages of paperwork, including a series of hypothetical situations with a paragraph-sized space for answering. Ava scanned the papers slowly. Question #12 "Student admits to cheating on previous exam. Please explain in detail the actions you would take."...#17 "Student asks for help with the following calculus problem: Please answer in paragraph format how you would explain the problem solving steps for this equation. Then select from the following mediums to complement your explanation: Power point diagram, bar graph, Excel chart, or stem and leaf plot. Explain the reason for your respective choice and how EXACTLY you would use chosen medium to accentuate your verbal explanation."

"Please have a seat at the table and fill out the paperwork completely. I will return in 30 minutes," said the short man in the black suit.

Ava sat down at the large oak table, took a deep breath, and began filling out the questionnaire. She thought about each question carefully and made a mental outline before she wrote a careful, neat answer. A couple of times she doubted herself and went back and read her answers again. Sometimes she read them out loud so she could hear what they sounded like. Exactly thirty minutes later the man in the black suit popped his head in the room and smiled. He looked at Ava, almost as if he were surprised she was still there. He walked in, gave her another smile and asked, "All set?"

Ava handed him the clipboard, now filled with her black ink handwritten answers to the many Educational Advantage essential questions. He glanced over her responses approvingly and then led her to a large conference room where she took a seat at the head of a large meeting table. A total of six interviewers sat on either side of her.

"Hi Ava," an older teacher-looking woman with wide rimmed glasses greeted her. She sat at the head of the table, not sure who to look at. She did her best to project confidence, but inside she felt overwhelmed and nervous. These six people were judging her and there she sat at the end, helpless. She felt like a piece of meat being attacked by six educated, eyeglass-wearing vultures. She was fighting for her life.

They each had a copy of her resume and asked questions like,

"What can you bring to Educational Advantage?"

"If Educational Advantage hired you how would you be an asset to the development of the company?"

It was harder getting into this agency than getting into college and probably almost as hard as getting a job at the FBI. Ava answered as best she could and went back and forth in her mind about what would happen if she got this job. She would be proud of herself. She would get to work with children. Her family would be very proud. It would look great on her resume. Then Ava thought about the possibility that she might not get it. She would be very, very disappointed.

"Where do you see yourself in five years and how does a job at Educational Advantage fit into this goal?"

"What do you hope to gain personally and professionally as an employee of Educational Advantage?"

At the end of the interview, Ava thanked these six individuals for grilling her and walked back out to the first office. The man in the black suit greeted her again and said,

"Thanks for coming Ms. Fleet. Please expect a call from us in one to three days."

"Thanks for eating me alive," Ava thought to herself as she shook his hand and walked out of the office. She left the large brick building and walked out into the sunny Los Angeles Thursday afternoon. The morning clouds had burned off and the afternoon sky was clear and beautiful. It was 5 o'clock and a text message on Ava's cell phone informed her that her girlfriends were laying out by the pool and drinking margaritas at Evan Shapiro's house. Funny how everyone had cell phones these days. Ava had even seen the cleaning lady at her sorority talking on hers. In fact, on the corner of Westwood Boulevard this very moment Ava swore she saw a homeless lady talking on her cell phone. Where did the bill go if she lived in Westwood Park in a box? Hmmm.

Anyway, the party sounded like just what Ava needed after three hours at Educational Advantage.

2

It was 79 degrees and poolside at Evan's house was the typical college party. Evan was one of these UCLA boys who grew up in LA, went to school, and still lived at home; after all, why trade in luxury and a desirable zip code for a college dormitory and repulsive food? Anyway, at least Evan was generous enough to share his parents' luxurious residence with the rest of his average college friends.

The keg flowed freely and Evan himself was at the barbeque, grilling up hot dogs and burgers for everyone. Evan was the richest and best-looking guy at UCLA.

"Watch out!" Demetri "Meat" Collins yelled as his 250-pound body cannonballed into the pool.

"Shit, Meat!" yelled Evan, his grill sizzling from the enormous splash from the pool.

Recovering from the blow and looking up to see Ava walking into the party amid all the ruckus, Evan cracked a smile and reached out his tan buffed out arm.

"Ava, my girl! Hey, Meat, get your fat ass over here and mix this girl up a margarita!"

"Thanks, Evan," Ava said.

"What's wrong, girl?" he asked, acknowledging the exhausted look on Ava's face.

"Oh, nothing, I just had a long job interview," she said, "There were six people asking me questions. I hardly knew which one to look at or what to say. I also had to fill out a whole long questionnaire. I could barely see after I filled everything out. I felt like I was explaining to them why I should live and not die. I think I did ok, but I'm not sure. I really want this job, and after that two hour interview, I really hope I get it."

"Tell me about it," Evan said, "I am interning at my dad's company and it is like, the worst. I mean, every morning I am like staring out the window, like thinking how much more productive I could be. I could be in the sauna detoxing or planning a dope summer trip. Instead I am entrusting my personal assistant to plan the whole thing and it is like, seriously freaking me out, but I just don't have the time right now," Evan said with a sigh. Then, suddenly remembering that the same rowdy group at his pool now would soon be transported to daddy's time share in Cabo, his head shot up and asked, almost panicking, "You are coming, right, girl?"

"Of course I am," said Ava.

"Whew, I was worried there for a minute," he said. Ah, the worries and stresses of a UCLA football star taking four units and interning at Daddy's company two days a week. His attitude was comical and he was quite a find for whichever girl eventually snagged him, and, trust and believe, he had his choice of females. His muscular, tanned body and scruffy brown hair were irresistible. However, every time any girl looked into his deep green eyes and laughed at one of his jokes, they were as good as gone. Evan was always the life of the party, and made it his number one priority that his group of friends were never lacking a fun time. His eight-figure trust fund was also quite charming. Evan's daddy had come to LA forty years ago with nothing and turned a job at the mailroom of Davis-McGrath into a partnership with the biggest management firm in town. Evan and Ava had been friends since elementary school, and had remained close friends through the LA private high school system and now at UCLA.

Meat brought over Ava's margarita, his chubby wet body stumbling along the side of the pool.

"Bottoms up!" he yelled.

"Dude, Meat, could you like not slobber all over Ava. It's like borderline nauseating, man." Evan scolded him.

"Huh, huh, sorry dude," Meat replied, snorting.

Ava shot him a smile to let him know it was really no big deal. He smiled back and walked back to the pool, a little less crazily.

"Where did you find him?" Ava asked.

Evan continued flipping burgers and replied, "Oh Meat's dad is a big actor and my dad is managing him now. My dad wants me to like, break him into the Kappa Alpha swing of things, you know. But he like, needs, serious help, obviously. I mean, he's like a complete mess, you see. Can you believe his dad is Angelo Pratt?"

"No!" screamed Ava, and then covered her mouth, embarrassed.

Angelo Pratt was the sexiest older man in Hollywood. He had a fantastic, sexy Richard Gere-Harrison Ford thing about him and he was married to Gianna Sanders, heiress to the apple juice fortune and a supermodel. How in the world did they produce such a child?

"I know," replied Evan, rolling his eyes, "What happened?"

Ava walked into Evan's pool house and used the restroom to change into her red and white polka dotted bikini. She then chose a chair poolside next to Bobbi Francis, her fellow sorority sister and roommate. Bobbi was thin and gorgeous, every fraternity boy's fantasy. She had big fake breasts that had been done by "the best plastic surgeon in all of LA." She had long blonde hair, like Ava. However, Ava did not always have hers perfectly done like Bobbi. Bobbi spent a lot of time in the gym with her personal trainer and talking on one of her two cell phones. Ava and Bobbi had met in their freshman year of college, in Anthropology 1. When they both moved into their sorority house their sophomore year, they were each other's obvious choice for a roommate. Ava was never home because she was always at the library, and Bobbi liked having the phone and room to herself most of the time. Ava was too worried about her grades to decorate their room, and Bobbi liked having the freedom to decorate the whole thing herself in leather and animal prints with pink trim, without someone giving her their opinion. Ava was not really a part of Bobbi's social scene, so Bobbi liked having Ava to tell all of her secrets to and gossip about her friends with. They were a good match; two opposites who fit each other like two puzzle pieces.

"I'm glad your husband THE LIBRARY let you out of the house today!" Bobbi said sarcastically. She was always giving Ava grief about not showing up at social events.

"Thanks, Bobbi. He told me to tell you he misses you," Ava replied.

Ava had brought Bobbi to the library once. She mostly whispered into her cell phone in a corner. She also walked up and down the library's seven flights of steps about ten times that night. "See, Ava, you can workout any time, anywhere!" she declared that night at 1:30 am, as Ava had her face buried in her Shakespeare book.

Ava and Bobbi laid in the sun next to each other. Ava dozed off as Bobbi was telling her some story about a new guy she met while shopping on Robertson. Some soap opera star on whom she had had a big crush FOREVER. As Ava fell asleep, she thought about Bobbi and all the other kids at the party. Parents stress going to college as being of the utmost importance. If parents only knew what really went on; that their hard-earned dollars were flowing out of a keg and into the mouths of horny sorority sisters and fraternity brothers. Most of Ava's friends thought getting an invitation to the Playboy Mansion was a bigger accomplishment than graduating with honors.

The party went on until the sun went down and everyone had changed back into jeans. The party grew bigger by nighttime, and by midnight there were two hundred UCLA fraternity brothers and sorority sisters boozing the night away and listening to music.

3

$\mathcal{A}$va awoke the next morning with a hangover tongue, but proud she had at least made it home in good-enough shape to wash her face, apply moisturizer, and brush her teeth the night before. She was exhausted but managed to put on her sweats and make it to her 10:00 am Shakespeare discussion.

Class crept by, and by the end of the fifty-minute discussion, Ava had finished her coffee and was back to normal. She headed to the library to review her notes before her statistics quiz at 2:00.

She walked through the quad, and ran into several attendees of Evan's party the night before. She waved at a boy she had seen as she was leaving last night, who had been closing in on a deal with her sorority sister Bobbi Francis. Ava smiled at him, and they gave each other that look, like "I know where you were last night." As she headed up the steps to the library, her cell phone rang.

"Hello."

"Hi, Ava Fleet please," the deep male voice on the other end inquired.

"This is Ava."

"Hi, Ava, this is Dr. Peters from Educational Advantage. Congratulations! We would like to offer you a position with our company. Can you come in Monday at noon for a short workshop and to receive your first assignment?"

Trying to hold back her excitement, Ava coolly answered, "Um, yes, Monday at noon is fine. Thanks."

"Ok, Ava, see you then. Welcome to Educational Advantage."

Ava snapped her phone shut and smiled. She was relieved more than proud for having endured the six-person, two-hour interview and coming up with a positive result. This was a great opportunity. She was happy to have a job that she thought she would enjoy and would involve helping children. She looked forward to her meeting on Monday.

4

*M*onday at 7:30 am Ava walked briskly out of the Kappa Kappa Gamma sorority house on Hilgard Avenue. Her long blonde hair was tied back in a ponytail and the ends were still slightly wet. She wore a gray fitted skirt that accentuated her curvaceous hips. She hid her busty chest again underneath a loose fitting red and white striped turtleneck sweater. She wore only mascara and light pink lip-gloss. She held her eight books for her classes today in an over-the-shoulder red Le Sportsac bag.

The sun was shining brightly in Ava's face as she crossed Hilgard to Le Conte Avenue. On the way, she passed two jogging sorority sisters who slowed down to wave and say hello.

"I should do that after this," Ava thought to herself.

Ava went to her morning classes and by 11:30 am, she was walking down Westwood Boulevard on her way to Educational Advantage. She walked into the front door of Educational Advantage and walked directly up to the receptionist to let her know she had an appointment. This time, the receptionist welcomed her and smiled and said,

"Yes, Ava Fleet, Dr. Peters is expecting you." The receptionist was a large black woman in her mid thirties and when she laughed it was as if the whole room laughed with her. She had a long brown ponytail and pretty green eyes. Her face was like sunshine, glowing and welcoming.

Before Ava had even taken a seat, the man in the dark suit from Thursday opened the office door. "Hello, Ava," he said, "Welcome back. I'm Dr. Peters. Can I get you anything? Coffee? Juice? Water?"

"Hi, oh no, I'm fine, well maybe some water," she replied, surprised at how obliging he was, considering his serious, stiff demeanor the other day. Ava had been accepted and had the approval of Educational Advantage.

He smiled a big welcoming smile and his bald head shone in the light when he turned around to lead Ava down a long hallway. His forehead wrinkled a lot when he talked and he had a strange nervous twitch in his right eye.

He led her to the same room with the big oak table and handed her a clipboard with only two papers on it. He held out his hand and showed her to a seat. He took a seat across from her, looked at her and then got up and made sure the door was closed.

"Well, Ava, welcome to Educational Advantage. Our panel was very impressed by your answers and your interview."

"Thanks," replied Ava.

"Well, Ava, let's begin. As you know, Educational Advantage is the most exclusive tutoring agency in town. We cater to very wealthy families, and we are proud of the reputation we have developed over the past twenty years. As a tutor working for us, you represent Educational Advantage, and we expect the tutors we hire to uphold our superior reputation."

Ava nodded and acknowledged Dr. Peters' every word. He spoke slowly. "Parents pay our exclusive fees and they expect exclusive, superior service. You must face the unique family situations carefully and strategically and always keep a positive attitude."

Ava and Dr. Peters continued discussing the ins and outs of what Ava previously thought would be a basic after-school job. Ava filled out form after form, disclaimer after disclaimer, release after release, guideline after guideline, until her hand practically signed and initialed her name by itself. Finally, Dr. Peters handed Ava her tutoring schedule for her first week. She would start with three clients and pending her performance in week one, her client list would increase. Her schedule listed the families, the times, and a brief description of what each family's tutoring goals were.

Two of the last names on Ava's list were ones any media-consuming American would recognize in a heartbeat. Ava could not believe she was going to go inside of their houses and tutor their children. Paparazzi stood outside of these homes all day long, hoping for a shot of the residents in their pajamas or laying out by the pool nude. Ava was going to be invited and welcome inside. She was so nervous that she could feel her heart beat rapidly. She wanted to do a good job. After all, these people were trusting her with their children's minds.

5

Annabelle was the cutest fourth grader Ava had ever seen. Ava picked her up at the Foundation for Gifted Children, the most prestigious elementary school in town, at 3:00pm on Wednesday for the first meeting. Ava waited in the car line and went through the complicated security process that the Foundation enforced in order to pick up children. It was quite an elaborate process, even for an exclusive elementary school. Ava had to wait in her Volkswagen Cabriolet behind all the mothers' brand new SUVs, the occasional red convertible belonging to the recently divorced, the hybrid vehicle for the sporadic political figure or environmentalist parent, and of course the ten year old Toyotas and Chevrolets belonging to the maids and nannies. The line stretched around the corner and it seemed like more of a nightclub for parents than an after school pick up line. The moms leaned into each others' car windows, holding the hot new handbag of the season, and gabbing about what they bought while shopping at Fred Segal today, how little 2nd grade Timmy was excited about his trip to New York next week to go look at private art colleges, how Dareou was the guest trainer at Gymboree this week, and how Elisa the nanny had given baby Jaden skim milk instead of soy this morning so of course she'd had to be fired and, "Do you know of anyone good as I can't possibly go a day without help!"

Ava waited in The Pickup Line for fifteen minutes. As Ava waited patiently, she observed the most curious series of events. These women of The Pickup Line excitedly ran up to each other, kissed each other once on each cheek, and squealed as if they hadn't seen each other in ages, or at least since yesterday at The Pickup Line. They whispered and gossiped about missing Pickup Line members; "Well, Andrea Simon's maid is here today picking up her twins. I heard she went to Monte Carlo with her trainer!!!"

"No," gasped another Pickup Line mommy. "He's so hot. That lucky bitch."

"Well, guess who's the new bachelor on the market! Patricia Price was killed yesterday in a freak liposuction accident. So you know what that means!" said one jewelry-clad mommy to another.

"No way!" replied the other mommy, "Tony Price of Price Steel is 100% available!"

"Way!" said the first mommy, "I'll challenge you to a thousand dollar wager that I can get a date before you can!"

"We're on!" replied the second mommy, as she shook hands with her competitor.

Watching these manicured, bleached, polished mothers, Ava wondered, "Would they really be able to go a day without help?" Ava recognized a lot of these women from earlier in the day when she drove down Rodeo Drive and saw a group of fancy ladies sitting at a fancy sidewalk café nibbling on pasta and sipping red wine. There was not a wrinkle on their faces and their breasts looked like they were only nineteen years old. They were thin and muscular and dressed in the hottest new perfectly-matching outfits that were tailored to fit their statuesque bodies. Although they all had small children and some even had new babies, they were perfectly clean. No macaroni and cheese on these Versace sweat suits. Not a single baby handprint on these white leather Louis Vuitton bags. Peanut butter and jelly on these cashmere sweaters? - NEVER!

"What do they do all day?..." Ava wondered to herself. She was genuinely intrigued.

Suddenly her daydreaming was interrupted and a curly haired brunette woman dressed in a blue striped sweater and jeans leaned over and looked at the sign Ava held which read "ANNABELLE SMITH" in big red letters on Foundation letterhead. The lady pulled down her sunglasses, and chomping on her gum, gave her a once over, and then as her mark of approval, turned around and yelled Annabelle's name into her megaphone.

A few seconds later a pony-tailed Annabelle came running out, wearing a big green backpack filled with so many books it looked as if she were embarking on a backpacking trip through Europe. She looked like one of the perfectly-crafted porcelain dolls that upscale toy stores kept in glass cases. Her hair was long and brown and tied up with a big puffy red rubber band. She was a beautiful little girl, but dressed like somewhat of a tomboy. She wore baggy jeans with a lot of pockets and bright red tennis shoes that lit up when she walked. Annabelle walked over to the car, looked inside a bit hesitantly, opened her braces-filled mouth and then asked, "Are you Ava?"

"Hi, yes I am," Ava smiled and said.

"OK," said Annabelle. She opened the passenger side door to the backseat, and plopped her enormous backpack on the backseat. The backpack took up enough space for two more Annabelles, and Ava had to turn around and lay the bag flat so that she could see out the back window. On the drive to her house, Annabelle flipped radio stations every three seconds, and when she heard the familiar tune of the Backstreet Boys, took her hand off the tuner and sang along to every word.

Annabelle didn't talk that much on the drive from West Hollywood to the flats of Beverly Hills. She sang along to the music and looked out the window. Ava thought she seemed like a happy little girl on the outside, but a bit sad on the inside.

They pulled up to Annabelle's house in the exclusive block of Maple Drive, an enormous white colonial home with a perfectly-manicured lawn and prize-winning rose bush. Ava had driven by this house before, and always wondered who lived inside, as everything about it was flawless. Annabelle opened her door and grabbed her green giant backpack. They walked in the side door.

Annabelle led them over to a breakfast nook in the kitchen, sat down, and pointing at a middle aged Latina woman, "This is Olivia," she said.

Olivia wore a traditional maid's outfit; a light blue dress and white ruffled apron. She smiled at them but before she was able to ask, Annabelle piped up, "Lox on a toasted sourdough bagel with light cream cheese, capers and sliced red onions, and a bottle of Pellegrino."

"Yes, miss," replied Olivia in a Spanish accent. "And for your teacher?"

"Just water, please," Ava said.

"Evian, Pellegrino, ice, no ice?" she asked.

Ava thought about this for a second. She always thought a glass of water was just a glass of water. Who knew there were so many choices?

"Evian, no ice, please," Ava replied.

With a snack on the way, Annabelle took her monogrammed Louis Vuitton notebook out of her green giant backpack, and examined a few silver Tiffany pens before settling on the one with which to embark on her homework. As Annabelle excavated these items, Ava surveyed the Smith house and could not find a speck of dust anywhere in sight. The picture frames were all expensive silver from Tiffany's and they were filled with photos of Annabelle and her dad: Annabelle and her dad at a horseshow, Annabelle and her dad on their yacht, Annabelle and her dad at a birthday party.

Her father was a tall, blonde, handsome older gentleman. He wore fancy polo shirts in all the photos. Hanging on the walls in the kitchen were countless movie posters signed by the stars themselves. They said things like, "Stan Smith - King of Showbiz xoxox Goldie Hawn," and "Stan the Man - Thanks for everything - Quentin Tarantino." Annabelle's father was obviously a very successful mover and shaker. Ava could tell by the looks of the photos in the kitchen that he, Olivia, and Annabelle were the only residents of this home.

Annabelle began her math homework and whizzed through it, only asking a couple of questions. As Ava was explaining a math equation to her, a sunglassed, tan, whistling dad walked through the door and into the kitchen, carrying a bag from Niketown. He punched his daughter playfully on the shoulder. "When you're done, Daddy's got a little surprise for his Annie from Niketown!" he teased. His big smile suddenly turned business like as he gazed over at Ava and looked her up and down. "And you are..."

"Hi, I'm Ava, the tutor," Ava replied.

"Right, of course. I'll need to talk to you when you're done," he said, matter-of-factly.

Ava nodded and continued with Annabelle as he walked upstairs.

The hour flew by and at exactly 4:15, Annabelle declared, "OK time's up, go talk to my dad so I can get my shoes!"

Ava walked up the two flights of stairs, past several portraits of Annabelle, and finally got to the first room on the right, where Olivia had directed her.

Ava knocked on the door and heard Mr. Smith's deep voice, "Come in."

Ava walked into his bedroom, which was much more masculine looking than the rest of the house. There was a big white bear rug, wood furniture, and a big four-poster bed with a tan comforter, and on top of the comforter, Mr. Smith lay on his back with his arms crossed behind his head. He smiled a sexy smile that gave Ava the chills. Ava did not want to make any presumptions, but she felt uncomfortable. "Have a seat on the edge of my bed and tell me about my Annie," he said in a tone not very father like, but in a way that Ava felt like they could have been sitting in a dark smoky bar talking over red wine and he had said," Come tell me about yourself."

Ava told Mr. Smith that she and Annabelle had worked on her math and that Ava thought Annabelle was advanced for her grade, that she understood the concepts well and that she could use more help reviewing...

"Now, what do you do?" Mr. Smith interrupted Ava as if suddenly his Annabelle was not as important or as interesting as was what was sitting on his bed.

"Um, I'm a tutor," Ava said matter of factly. What the fuck did he think she was? The local prostitute cleverly disguised as a tutor?

His eyes asked for more so Ava continued, "I am an English major at UCLA and I hope to one day work in..."

Suddenly he touched her arm. His palm was big and sweaty. He had a simple gold band on his wedding finger,

28

which for a split second made Ava think, "Where is Annabelle's mother?" His white collared shirt was wrinkled and his maroon paisley tie hung loosely around his neck. Ava could see that his face was more wrinkled than she had thought, now that she was up close to him. However, he was sexy in an older Michael Douglas kind of way. Ava felt his warm breath on her cheek and smelled a hint of Old Spice. The muscles in his arm were athletic and tan. He had light blonde hair on his arms, but barely any. He had a peculiar looking birthmark on the inside of his elbow; it looked like a lima bean. His lips were soft looking, but Ava could tell he was a skier by the slight wind-chapped redness of them. His eyes were light green and distant. Breaking the uncomfortable silence he had created, those eyes looked deeply into Ava's as he said, "I think you and Annabelle will get along well. By the way, Olivia and I think you're very beautiful."

"Um, thanks," Ava replied as she got up quickly and, acting as if nothing had happened, waved goodbye and said, "Bye, Mr. Smith, see you tomorrow!"

"Please call me Stan," he said in his deep sexy voice.

Ava ran down the stairs and waved goodbye to Annabelle and Olivia. She walked out the front door and as she headed to her car, a beautiful blonde woman drove up in a bright red, shiny Mercedes. She parked in the Smith driveway, got out of the car and waved at Ava. "Hi, you must be the tutor I hired!" she said with a big smile. She was a beautiful lady. She wore a white pants suit and gold shoes. She wore big pearl earrings and a large pearl necklace to match. "I'm sorry I couldn't make it in time to meet you. I hope Stan was able to explain everything all right," she said. "I've just been so busy. I was at the florist, the baker, such a hectic day," the woman explained, shaking her head. "I'm trying to plan this charity event. I'm just way over my head. By the way, I'm Pamela, Stan's ex-wife," she said as she shook Ava's hand and laughed hysterically. It was all very confusing to Ava. Pamela Smith knew that and felt sorry for the girl. She was so young and inexperienced. Pamela had been through it all with Stan. They tried getting married before, when they were very young. Things had seemed like they could have been so perfect then. At least Pamela wanted to make it that way. She knew her husband had a wandering eye. In the beginning, she wanted to tame him, but she soon realized it would have been easier teaching an armadillo to cook Beef Wellington. She had been angry at first, divorced him and demanded half of everything. However, over the years, she had grown to understand his ways, and now she accepted them rather than tried to fight them. They were a bizarre couple, living in two separate houses, jointly taking care of their two children and Annabelle, Stan's child from his second marriage. It was odd, but it worked for them. She knew his agenda, and he knew hers. In an unconventional way, things had worked out.

However, Ava could only offer this woman a blank face as she stood in front of her. "Well, nice to meet you," Pamela said with a big smile, "See you next time."

"Yes, nice to meet you, Pamela," Ava replied with a smile.

Ava walked to her car and took a deep breath as she put the keys in the ignition and started the car. She had 11 minutes to get to her next student in Bel Air. Hopefully her next meeting would be a little less eventful. As Ava drove, she thought about Pamela, Stan, Olivia, and Annabelle, and what a strange family they were. Ava had a lot of respect for Pamela Smith. She was beautiful and everything about her was perfect. Her nails were French-manicured and her hair looked like it had just been professionally done. She spoke eloquently and gracefully and she stood tall and confident. Ava sat up a little straighter as she drove and imagined that she was driving home to her beautiful house, with a white picket fence, a 90210 zip code, and a closet full of designer clothes.

6

$\mathcal{It}$ was nearly 4:30 when Ava drove through the Bel Air West Gate. She took Bel Air Road to Rocca Way and drove up the steep hill until she reached a castle-like structure belonging to the Johnson family. Ava drove past two colossal pillars, and felt as though she had driven from Bel Air back to the Middle Ages. A moat surrounded the large gray stone structure. A heavy wood and metal bridge led one over the moat and into the large sturdy structure. There were six garages. The garage doors were made of the same heavy wood and metal material as the bridge. Ava drove across the moat and onto a large open concrete area closed in by tall golden gates. In this large open area were parked at least ten luxury cars, all of which were fixed up with every kind of amenity. A brand new convertible red Mercedes SL 500 was parked in front. The upholstery on the chairs inside was a leopard leather print. Leopard print fuzzy dice hung from the rearview mirror. Next to it was parked a black Lincoln Navigator with leather interiors, and the biggest stereo system Ava had ever seen. The entire front of the house was lined with similar cars. All of them were so shiny and clean that you could eat off them. They all were decked out beyond belief.

Ava awkwardly parked her Volkswagen Cabriolet in the middle of all these gaudy cars, and walked toward the front door of the house. She could hear loud rap music blasting from the inside. The bass was so loud and deep, the windows were shaking. Emblazoned on the door in bright gold was the letter "Z." Ava knocked on the large metal knocker but no one answered. All she could hear was the sound of bass shaking the whole house. Ava knocked again and suddenly heard what sounded like 10 presumably huge dogs growling deeply.

The door slowly opened and there stood a tall, skinny man wearing a long Lakers jersey, a red bandana on his head, and brand new tennis shoes. "'Sup?" he said and nodded his head at Ava.

The he turned around and yelled behind his back, "Little Z, yo teacher!"

He walked away and left Ava standing at the door. The loud rap music continued and, standing on the front steps in her pink collared shirt, knee length white denim skirt, cream heels, and black backpack, Ava's whole body pulsated to the music. She stuck out like a sore thumb. Since she was standing at the door alone, she decided to remove her pink hairband and take down her ponytail. She ran her hand through her long blonde hair to straighten it out. Her hand shook from the strength of the bass as she touched her head. The music was so loud it was almost as if she were sitting in one of those massage chairs at The Sharper Image on full blast.

After several minutes of standing on the front porch, in front of the backdrop of luxurious, pimped-out vehicles, Ava heard footsteps coming toward her, presumably of at least three people. A young boy, who looked about ten years old, strolled to the front door with his hand in the air. His long shiny bright red t-shirt nearly blinded Ava. For all she knew, it was only a t-shirt walking towards her, as a blue baseball cap and aviator sunglasses covered the boy's head and eyes. His big white tennis shoes looked too big for his feet, and the diamond and gold jewelry on his fingers and around his neck was more than Ava had ever seen anyone wear, man or woman. Two beautiful, voluptuous women flanked this little man. On the left was a blonde in a hot pink skintight cat suit and leopard stiletto heels. She had one hand on the little man's shoulder and another on her curvy hip. On the other side of him stood another voluptuous beauty, but a brunette with dark olive skin. She wore a short black dress and black stiletto heels. Her dark green cat eyes stared at Ava as she smoked a cigarette and sipped a glass of champagne. They were a sight to see, and standing at their feet were two large bull mastiffs, wearing black leather spiked collars and growling. Their fur was shiny, and, like everything else in the house, they looked like they had just been cleaned.

The little man and his entourage walked toward Ava. The little man smiled, as the two ladies posed next to him.

"Word, I'm Z. You're my teacher?" he said.

"Hi, I'm Ava, the tutor."

"Cool, welcome to the crib," he smiled. "Ladies, meet Ava."

Little Z's two counterparts smiled without showing their teeth and didn't say a word. The bullmastiffs growled. Little Z shouted something in what sounded like German, and the two dogs walked slowly away, hanging their heads down.

Ava followed Little Z and the two ladies down the hallway and into Little Z's room. His bed looked like a throne. The headboard was gold and the bedspread dark maroon velvet, piled with animal print pillows. Platinum records hung on the wall. Pictures of Little Z lined the walls as well. There was a painting over the bed of Little Z looking like royalty. In the oil on canvas piece, he was sitting on a large velvet chair, holding a scepter and wearing a crown. Along the wall were photos of Little Z with an eclectic mix of people and circumstances: Little Z with Snoop Dog, Little Z with Quincy Jones, Little Z and Dr. Dre on a yacht, Little Z with Donald Trump and three beautiful young ladies, Little Z with Paris Hilton, Little Z and his father with Ja Rule, Little Z with President Clinton at Camp David.

Little Z took out a red shiny notebook and a pencil and slapped it on the bed.

"Alright, I got to pass eighth grade. If I pass, I make it into high school. My record is blowing up and I don't have time for school, but pops says if I want to tour this summer, I need to pass. You're gonna help me, right?"

"We are going to help each other," Ava said. "You will help me understand what you need help with and I am going to help you learn it."

35

"Word, so let's get crackin'," Little Z declared as he hopped up on the bed and snapped his fingers. His two voluptuous beauties exited the room.

Little Z was a motivated student. This made Ava very happy, as sometimes the toughest part of this job was getting the students excited about their work. Little Z already wanted to learn.

Ava looked around the room. "Why don't we sit at your desk, Little Z?"

"Word"

Ava took out a review book from her bag. She placed it on the desk and Little Z snatched it out of her hand and began flipping through the pages and nodding his head. "Ok, I can learn this."

"Let's begin with math," Ava said.

"Nah, nah, I'm cool with math. English is my problem."

Ava flipped to the English section and began reading a passage with Little Z.

"Hold up," said Little Z as he reached into his desk drawer and grabbed five different color highlighters. He took a highlighter in each hand and began highlighting different parts of the story as he read along. Suddenly a buzzing, vibrating noise came from inside the desk. Little Z abruptly put down the highlighters and yanked open the desk drawer to reveal five cell phones in different colors: red, blue, purple, yellow, and green. He picked each one up separately and shut them off.

"Sorry," Little Z said, "cannot be distracted while getting my learn on."

Little Z moved quickly. It was almost as if he was racing himself to see how much he could learn in as little time as possible.

"Just out of curiosity, Little Z, why do you need so many phones?" Ava asked. She had just bought herself one after researching all the different prices and plans, and she knew that one was expensive enough.

"One for family, one for friends, one for girls, one for business, and the red one that lights up-that one's for my moms," Little Z explained.

Ava and Little Z read through the entire English section quickly, all the while Little Z made notes to himself. He drew all kinds of graffiti over his piece of paper, until he had filled three whole pieces with images that resembled ones that gangsters wrote on the side of freeway onramps.

As Ava watched over Little Z's studying, her eyes scanned the room and stopped dead on a remarkable photo of Tupac Shakur holding what appeared to be Little Z as a baby dressed in flashy gold and diamond jewelry and a jersey style shiny t-shirt. "Little Z, that picture of Tupac is amazing. You were so lucky to meet him before he died. The way he used syllables, onomatopoeia, and alliteration in his writing! He was such a wordsmith. I think his work is phenomenal. It changed the way I think about the English language."

Little Z stared at Ava as though she had just said something in Japanese. Then he smiled and said, "Homeboy could rap!"

"Good idea, Tutor. This party could use some beats." Little Z yanked open the desk drawer and took out a silver remote control. He pointed at a wall in his room and all of a sudden, the wall folded out and flipped around to reveal a stereo system that looked like something that belonged in a nightclub. The sound of Tupac's rapping filled the room. Little Z turned down the volume so the music was only background for the study session. Little Z tapped his foot and sang along. "Hail Mary is such a dope rhyme."

Ava saw that Little Z's enthusiasm about Tupac could be translated into his English work. If she could somehow show Little Z that Tupac's writing was poetry, too, then Little Z would understand his English.

"Yeah, that one's alright, "Ava said, "but I really like '96 Bonnie and Clyde."

"How do you know so much about the Pac experience?" Little Z asked as he laughed at her a little bit.

"I love him, "Ava said, "He's the shit."

Little Z flew back in his chair, wiped his brow as his mouth dropped wide open. "Damn, Tutor, you are some woman...smart and you like rap. I wanna wife you. Let's get married."

"Very funny, Little Z. I have a better idea, let's pass eighth grade," Ava said.

Little Z continued to memorize grammar and vocabulary, all the while making all kinds of graffiti. Ava did not question his writing, until the end. When they had come to the last section, Ava praised, "Little Z, you are a phenomenal artist."

"Word, I know," he said, smiling a big smile.

"What exactly is it for?" she asked him.

"It's my code, to remember."

"Great," said Ava, "Codes are always a really good trick for remembering information."

The afternoon with Little Z went smoothly. In fact, Ava even stayed an extra half hour, after Little Z begged her to go over the practice English test once more until he got a 95% instead of a 93%. "I got to get all this down," he kept saying. He was a very determined young man and although Ava had just met him, she was already proud of him. She felt like she had already helped him and he was learning.

As Ava was leaving, Little Z handed her a special promotional package with a Little Z beanie, a Little Z t-shirt, and Little Z's new album, "LITTLE Z:Get Yer ZZZs."

"Check out my new tracks, especially I think you would like number 11," said Little Z, with a big gold-toothed smile.

Then as Ava was walking out the large wooden front door and back on the bridge and over the moat, Little Z panicked, "When are you coming back????"

As Ava turned around, she saw that the two voluptuous women had resumed their positions on either side of Little Z and the two bull mastiffs stood directly in front of him, growling in a bit more friendly way now that Ava had been approved.

"Um, tomorrow 6:00?"

"6:30, I have my trainer from 5:00-6:00," Little Z said, "and then I need to get my learnin' supplies ready for you."

Not sure what exactly that meant, Ava shrugged her shoulders. "Ok, great, see you tomorrow Little Z."

"You can call me Zeus," he said, as he took off his hat, put it on his chest, and smiled a fantastic million-dollar smile. His two voluptuous ladies giggled a little bit as Ava walked to her car and drove down and out of Bel Air.

7

$\mathcal{A}$va returned to Little Z's house the next day at 6:30 pm sharp. She drove halfway up the long driveway but was stopped dead in her tracks, as she was blocked by a large Staples freight truck. Ava backed out the driveway and parked on the street. She walked back up the long driveway and around the delivery truck.

Little Z was endlessly barking commands, "Yo, everything goes to the office on the first floor. And you guys got to arrange the shit, you know, like pencils in the cup, paper in the first drawer, set up the fax, internet, get it all ready to rock."

As Ava walked into Little Z's sight, he held up his hand to salute her. "Yo, tutor, what up????!!!!!" Then Little Z got serious. "All right, we have so much going on here. Do you prefer Mac or PC?" Little Z asked with the seriousness of a doctor asking for a blood type before a blood transfusion.

All the people and things at Little Z's house over-whelmed Ava. It was as though Little Z was setting up FBI headquarters. How nice of him to offer her a computer to use!

41

"Either one, Little Z," she replied, "I like both."

"Alright, 2 Macs, 2 PC. Put all the snacks in the cupboard behind the desk," Little Z barked at the three workmen from Staples who were unloading desks, chairs, a fax machine, a paper shredder, computers, boxes of supplies and electric cords, and boxes of snacks: red vines, pistachio nuts, soda, water. It was enough for Little Z to transport his entire class into his own home and conduct school at his house.

"Now we are really ready to roll, Tutor!" Little Z exclaimed.

"Wow, Little Z, do we really need all this stuff?" Ava asked him.

"Yep, of course, now we are fully prepared to learn. We both have computers, fax machine, and snacks to keep our brains working. Remember, you help me, I help you, right?"

"Right, Little Z, that's right!" Ava said.

Little Z led Ava into an office downstairs that was now being set up by the three Staples workmen. Within a few minutes, everything was done.

A Staples workman walked over to Little Z and handed him a clipboard with his bill on it. Little Z signed on the dotted line with a big fancy "Z". Then Little Z handed each workman a crisp "c-note" $100 bill.

Ava and Little Z sat down, side by side at brand new

large oak desks, more fitting for two studio executives than a tutor in a sundress and a 14 year old student. Ava took her tattered GED review book out of her large red bag and opened it to the English section again.

Little Z shot up, ran across the room and grabbed a red book and a brand new CD ROM wrapped in cellophane.

"Tutor, I got CD ROM. More pimp, more faster!"

Ava put her tattered GED book away, ashamed that she had not provided her student with the best technology. She felt lucky to be employed by such an enthusiastic student who was obviously making big waves in the music world. She felt badly, like she should have done better and brought him a CD ROM instead of an old book.

"Great Little Z, I am so happy that you are so excited about learning! " she said.

"Oh, I almost forgot!" Little Z said. He pulled out the drawer of the new desk and took out a silver remote control and pointed it at the wall. The wall flipped around, just like in his bedroom, and revealed a monstrous stereo system. Tupac was playing, the CD ROM was in the computer, and the studying was rolling along at full blast.

Little Z whipped through more reading passages and reading comprehension questions, but when they got to poetry, Little Z let a frown creep across his face.

"Poetry is whack, I don't get it, " he said.

"Little Z, what are you talking about????? You are a rapper, poetry should be your favorite!"

"Nah, Tutor, rap is one thing, but this fruity stuff about 'my heart is this' and 'art thou lonely,' nope, it ain't the same!"

The room went silent. Ava shook her head. "Little Z, I am very disappointed in you."

"Sorry Tutor, my rhymes equal dope, these rhymes equal opposite of dope."

"No, Little Z, that is not why I am upset. Think about what you just said."

Little Z gave Ava a look as if she again had said something in Japanese.

"Little Z, you said, 'It ain't the same!' What did we just learn about negatives?"

Little Z rolled his eyes and hit himself on the head. "Stupid Little Z! Pay attention to yo shit!, " he said, "It is not the same! It is not the same! It is not the same! It is not the same!"

"Thank you Little Z! Good job! But you don't need to punish yourself! You are learning and that is the most important thing!"

"Alright, alright," said Little Z, " but poetry is still whack!"

"Little Z, you love Tupac and I love Tupac, right?"

"May he rest in peace, " declared Little Z.

"So let's try to use your Tupac to learn your poetry."

"Word, how about Hail Mary?" Little Z asked.

Little Z jumped up out of the desk and ran across the room to a drawer underneath the stereo. He yanked out the drawer and pulled out a black piece of cloth. Little Z bent over and tied the black bandana onto his head so it was covering the top and front of his head. Then he stood up, crossed his arms in front of his chest, and closed his eyes. He took a deep breath in and raised his hands over his head.

"Number three please," he said seriously.

Ava picked up the silver remote and clicked it to play number three on the CD. Little Z began waving his hands in the air as the music played and rapped along to the music. "Come with me, Hail Mary, come with me." Little Z was engulfed by the music. Tupac filled his soul.

However, Ava saw the time passing and had to get Little Z to pay attention. "Good work, Little Z," Ava said, "Now let's think about the words to the song and what they mean."

"I got the words, Tutor, signed by Pac himself."

Little Z walked into the other room and came back a minute later with a gold plaque. It was a framed copy of Tupac's original lyrics, handwritten on lined paper and signed with a gold pen, "**To:Z, Peace, Pac**"

"I was just a pup when he gave it to me," Little Z said, shaking his head solemnly.

"OK Little Z, look at what you are holding in your hand. It IS poetry. Read it out loud."

Little Z read the words aloud and realized that they rhymed, just like some of the Shakespeare poems he had been reading before.

Little Z nodded. "Word, I guess he is a little like Shakespeare."

With that, Ava and Little Z began reading the poetry section of his English book. Little Z was a quick learner and used his Tupac song to learn different poetry terms and then applied them to his poetry. Ava was proud of him. He was so motivated and she really felt useful when she was at his house helping him. She was helping him learn and he was ever-appreciative. She even had to remind him when their time was up. He asked her to stay late when she said, "OK, Little Z, that's it for today."

"No! No! No! I was just getting on a roll and now you're gonna bounce? Come on!" he said, frustrated.

"Little Z, I wish I could stay but I have to do my homework, too! I'm sorry. I will be back tomorrow again. After the trainer."

"Nah, that's cool, T, I forgot I have a interview tonight," he said, "Alright Tutor. Thanks. I learned a grip today." With that, Little Z tore himself away from his studying and walked Ava to the door. On the way out he grabbed Ava's hand and handed her three crisp c-notes.

"You the shit, Tutor," Little Z said, with a big smile. Ava couldn't believe the generous tip from Little Z. Three hundred dollars! She could buy all her textbooks for next quarter. She almost wanted to cry.

"Thanks, Zeus," she said.

As he walked away and Ava walked out the driveway, she could hear Little Z summon his twin beauties. "Double Trouble, where you at???"

Ava walked down the driveway and into the car and drove off, proud of Little Z for how dedicated he was to his work and what a determined young man he was. He was going to go far in life.

8

*W*ork was done, and Ava had her own work to do. She took her backpack, filled with books, to the University Center to do some studying. She treated herself to a fancy $4.00 coffee from the coffee shop and sat in the middle of the student center at a large table, big enough for four. She needed the space to spread out all her books and papers. The University Center was a good place to study. It was a huge common area with tables and a large TV that usually showed a program at low volume; just enough background noise. Ava didn't like to study in total silence.

She sat down and began to review for her History midterm. She turned the pages and took detailed notes. She wanted to do well in this class. It was interesting and it was not in her major requirements. She wanted to prove to herself that she could get a good grade. As she studied she heard the quiet lull of the TV, and then, suddenly, a familiar voice caught her attention. Ava looked up from her books to the big screen TV in the corner. There on 20/20, being interviewed by Barbara Walters, was Little Z himself, sitting in a plush red velvet throne, flanked by his two beautiful ladies, and wearing a jeweled crown.

"You know, Barbara, I'm really excited about my album. This is some of my best efforts. I employed my past experiences with my forward-thinking optimism for the future. I'm going into this tour with gratitude to God for the blessed life he's given me, and my heart is filled with prayers for an equally fortunate future," he said, quite prolifically, with his hands crossed in front of him.

Ava smiled. Little Z, what a lyricist. She was proud of him.

9

$\mathscr{A}$va arrived home to her sorority house just before dinner was over. She made herself a plate of salad, took a seat alone in the corner of the dining room, and opened her English book. She had more studying to do. She had been at class all day and then Little Z's house all afternoon and early evening. She had to get going on her studying.

She began reading the assigned pages in her *Paradise Lost* book and took notes. Suddenly she heard the giggling and laughing of several sorority girls.

"Baby, are you coming out?!" Bobbi squealed as she spotted Ava in the corner. Bobbi smelled like alcohol and was wearing Ava's pink shirt.

Ava smiled at the five girls who were headed out on their way to a party. "I wish, Bobbi, but I have too much work to do."

"Oh yeah, how's your new job?" Bobbi asked.

Ava bent down and began digging in her backpack for a different colored highlighter. "Oh it's cool. I just started, so we'll see," Ava began, "I think I'm doing okay, but I'll know when I get my first evalua..." Ava lifted her head up, and Bobbi was gone, off to a party in Ava's shirt.

She spent the rest of the evening studying. At 11:30, she went upstairs, brushed her teeth, and changed into her pajamas. She knelt down next to her bed and said her prayers. She prayed for her health and her family and thanked God for her blessings. She got in bed and drifted off to sleep. She didn't even wake up when Bobbi stumbled in at 3:00 am and passed out in her clothes, or rather Ava's shirt and her leather pants.

10

$\mathcal{A}$va drove carefully along Stone Canyon Road. She followed the numbers along looking for the Kurakis house. She passed the Bel Air Hotel and followed the road up.

Stone Canyon, 1200, 1206...ah 1230-1237 was a small gated community of their own. Ava pulled up to the kiosk and was greeted by a man in full security uniform.

"Good afternoon, miss, your name please."

"Ava Fleet," she replied.

The man flipped through a metal clipboard, turning several pages until he got to Ava's name and gave her an approving glance. "OK, Miss Fleet, we'll need your drivers license, proof of insurance, and social security card."

A little surprised at such an intricate screening process to enter a gate, Ava removed the cards from her wallet and handed them over to the officer, thinking this might be a joke. He took her documents to his small copy machine, copied them, and handed them back to her.

He then produced an electronic clipboard that looked like something between an Etch-A-Sketch and an electronic UPS signature box. He handed it to Ava through the car window. She looked at the small computer and saw her name on the screen in big bold letters, copies of her documents, a photo of herself handing the documents to the security officer from 2 minutes beforehand, and a blank box.

"Miss Fleet, please press your thumb into the blank box. We need fingerprints for our records," he instructed her.

She placed her thumb in the blank box and hoped this was the end of the process. She was then issued a badge with her name on it and a seal of approval stamp from the security officer.

"OK Miss Fleet, drive forward through the gate. When you get to the next checkpoint, show them your badge and photo id."

She drove through the gate and up a hill to another brick kiosk. This station, however, was filled with at least seven security cameras and a computer screen that flashed the same information as she saw before on the small screen. Another uniformed security guard greeted her.

Ava showed him her new badge and driver's license. The second security guard handed her a small paper map and drew directions on it with a red pen. Ava was overwhelmed with what an intricate process it was to get into this house. Two security checkpoints already. Ava was reminded of when she went to the White House with her family in the seventh grade. She decided it was definitely harder to get in here than in the house where the President of the United States lives.

"Go up the first hill, make a right on Woodley and pull up to the silver gate," the security guard said. She drove further up along the private drive until she reached a silver gate. She stuck her hand out of the car window and rang the call button.

"Hello," a voice answered.

"Hi this is Ava the tu- " BZZZZZZZZ !!! The large silver gates slowly opened towards her.

Ava pulled into the long circular driveway and parked her car in what felt like a showroom of impeccable, shiny luxury cars. She wondered if the people who lived here even really drove them. She walked past the grand fountain and up to the front door.

"Hubba hubba," an obnoxious voice said. "Hubba hubba," it said again.

Startled, Ava turned around and saw a beautiful macaw perched on a large branch next to the fountain. She laughed and then turned around suddenly when she heard the front door open. She abruptly stopped laughing when she saw what was in front of her.

A tall handsome young man answered the door. He must be the student's older brother. Maybe he was even a student at UCLA with Ava. He was tall, dark, and handsome, the classic "looker" who immediately took Ava's breath away. He was the guy in high school she always longed for but was too shy to meet. Seeing him made Ava angry about how mousy she was in high school. "Why did I ALWAYS wear my straight brown hair back in a boring ponytail? Why didn't I get my braces off before high school? I was always popular; I was an athlete and went to all the fun parties, but I wasn't the petite perky cheerleader, the Pamela Anderson of prep school," Ava thought to herself.

"Hi, I'm Jarrod Kurakis, you're my tutor?" he asked.

Ava's heart dropped. What a stroke of luck. Initially confused that this handsome specimen was a student Ava would be spending several hours per week with, she got over her hesitation and became rather excited at the prospect of being near something so beautiful for such a great amount of time. Ava looked at him and felt like she was walking on air. His tanned shoulders peeked out from under his torn tank top. He looked like a GQ angel, with perfect white teeth, blonde hair, and gleaming blue eyes. Ava couldn't believe he was only 17 years old. She stopped herself for a minute, when she realized that she was lusting after an under aged high school boy. However, he was only 3 years younger than she was. He made her nervous. She was suddenly reminded of high school when she had a big crush on the captain of the football team. His name was Brian Collins. She sat next to him in Geometry class and was sure to bring an over-supply of red pens, high-lighters, erasers, and pencils just in case he asked to borrow one. When she sat next to him then, she didn't have a volup-tuous, athletic body, but was a slightly chubby, unmade-up, baggy corduroy pants and baggy polo shirt wearing nerd. Their "romance" began when he asked to copy her homework. Eventually it developed into a beautiful meaningful relation-ship where he copied Ava's answers during tests. He was relieved and she was in heaven. Having Brian Collins copy her math answers was as close to having a real boyfriend as Ava Fleet ever got in high school. Ava loved it more than any-thing when she was walking through the halls alone, would walk past his group of popular football guys and scantily clad cheerleaders, and he would pop his head out of the circle and say, "Hi, Ava." His validation was just as good as a diamond ring as far as she was concerned. It was the one time during the day where she felt special. His little cheerleader friends always looked over at her frumpy figure walking through the halls and gave her a surprised look as if to say, "Um, and why is he saying hello to HER?" She enjoyed keeping their questions unanswered. She was the only one who knew why he was getting his A in geometry. To those cheerleader girls, she was a real live friend of Brian Collins!

So, now she sat standing in front of the reincarnated Brian Collins, about to spend some quality time with him. Suddenly a little brown haired boy ran up behind Jarrod and squirted him with his squirt gun, laughed, and then ran away. "Carson!!!!" Jarrod screamed at his younger brother.

"Sorry," Jarrod said, looking at Ava. "Come on, let's get started." They sat down at a large glass kitchen table and he took out his homework. He asked many questions and smiled at Ava often. He made her laugh and she wondered if he was flirting or that was just the way he spoke. The more time she spent with him, the more she realized she was developing a crush on this underage high school boy whose family had put her in their employ to pass his classes so he could get into the same university as his successful and intelligent Kurakis relatives. He joked about his own stupidity. After she spent twenty minutes with him explaining how to do a proof, he looked at her blankly.

"Ok, now you try number 13," she suggested.

He stared at Ava and busted up laughing. "Uh, yeah right," he said, laughing uncontrollably.

"Ok, let's try this again," she said, a bit frustrated at him thinking that his charm could win her over and she would dismiss the past twenty minutes she just spent explaining this to him.

He smirked at Ava and gave her the most heart-melting smile and said, "Is somebody upset? Does somebody have PMS?"

He made Ava laugh. She looked up and smiled at him.

As her eyes met his, suddenly a woman's loud cackling and the click clacking of high heels broke the silence. A tall, thin, busty, gorgeous blonde woman wearing a bright pink dress and clear stiletto heels emerged in the doorway. She wore dark sunglasses with large, diamond "Cs" on the side of them and carried at least seven glossy shopping bags from Neiman Marcus.

"Hi, baby!" she squealed at Jarrod as she placed one of the Neiman Marcus bags on the table.

"Hi, mom," Jarrod said in an annoyed, monotone voice.

"Don't be so grumpy, baby!" she squealed again and kissed him on the cheek. "Look inside the bag, Jarrod!" she insisted.

"Mom, I'm trying to study," Jarrod replied, rolling his eyes. "This is Ava, my tutor."

Frustrated that Jarrod would not look at this new gift, Angelica stuck out her hand. "Hi, I'm Jarrod's mom, Angelica Thurman," she said.

Ava was speechless. She thought this woman resembled Angelica Thurman, but she could not believe she was the "real" Angelica Thurman…the real, live, actual Angelica Thurman. Angelica Thurman was standing right here, within two feet of Ava. She was perfect. She must have been at least 36 years old, as Ava remembered seeing her movies when she was just a child. Angelica Thurman had won two Oscars and had been linked to so many Hollywood men. She had once dated Michael Douglas and for years was married to the head of a major studio. This was really her, standing right in front of Ava. Angelica Thurman was her boss.

"Hi," Ava replied, "Nice to meet you." Ava tried to act unimpressed, but she could hardly concentrate, she was so overwhelmed.

"What do you do, sweetie?" she asked Ava.

Ava hesitated. Was this some kind of trick question that every parent was going to ask? "I'm Jarrod's tutor," Ava replied.

"Oh right, ok," Angelica said, not seeming to care, as she tossed her hair around. Jarrod shook his head.

"Don't shake your head at me, Jarrod," Angelica said, sternly. "Now be a good boy and open the gift from mommy."

Jarrod reluctantly reached his hand into the glossy Neiman Marcus bag and pulled out a Jean Paul Gaultier top that was made of sheer white fabric and had a cartoon face on it. It was so small, it looked like it would fit Jarrod very snuggly.

"Do you like it baby?" she asked excitedly.

Judging by Jarrod's face, he wasn't very interested in this shirt.

"Thanks mom," he replied.

"So ungrateful, my boy," she said to Ava.

"So I'll just pay you now because I'm gonna take a bath." Angelica said.

She reached in her big black handbag and pulled out a hundred dollar bill and placed it on the table in front of Ava. Shocked, Ava piped up," Oh, Ms. Thurman, it's only $10 per hour, and you pay the agency directly."

Angelica didn't even know what it cost. Ava remembered when she was in school, she begged her parents for a tutor to help her study for her SAT. Her parents researched four different companies before hiring the cheapest one-and at a maximum of one hour per week. These Beverly Hills parents didn't even ask or care.

"Well, Jarrod is a big job, I'm sure you deserve a little more for working with us," she replied and then walked away from Jarrod and Ava, whistling to herself.

"Thank you," Ava said, staring in amazement at the hundred-dollar bill.

11

$\mathcal{I}t$ was Wednesday afternoon and Ava returned to the Smith house. Stan Smith's red Ferrari was not in the driveway. Ava walked to the front door and rang the bell. Ava heard the pitter patter of little feet and then the door opened. Annabelle stood in the doorway looking like the perfect child. Her hair was in two picture-perfect pigtails tied up by red rubber bands. She wore a red babydoll dress and delicate beige ballet slippers with two intertwined Cs on the front. Out of her perfect little shoes peeked white lace bobby socks. She was a flawless portrait of child perfection, except for the smear of chocolate across her porcelain face. She smiled big at Ava and exclaimed, "Olivia is making cookies! Want one?!?"

"Thank you," Ava said as she walked into the Smith house and followed Annabelle into the kitchen.

Olivia was watching Spanish soap operas and cutting up pieces of Teuscher chocolates. The large gold box that the chocolates came in sat open on the counter and the $73.00 price tag hung loosely from a thick, elegant ribbon. Next to the chocolates were shopping bags from a supermarket Ava had only been into once in her life. She had stopped there out of emergency when she was dying of thirst and bought only a bottled water. It was all a student like her could have bought in a supermarket where fancy ladies and Pickup Line mommies bought paper towels so elegant they could have doubled as bed sheets.

Annabelle reached into the shopping bag and pulled out a bag of organic flour.

"You help, tutor!" she said.

Ava, Olivia, and Annabelle poured, mixed, blended, and baked until they turned out a fabulous flawless dozen chocolate chip cookies. As they sat at the Smith family kitchen chomping on their culinary creation and drinking vanilla flavored soy milk, Ava calculated how fabulous exactly these chocolate chip cookies were. They had used a whole box of Teuscher chocolates, plus ingredients all from Gelson's supermarket and one small bottle of Evian....total divided by twelve....each cookie was worth about $13 and they were absolutely delicious.

As they sat at the table in the Smith family kitchen, in walked Pamela fresh from the facialist. Her face looked nothing short of a pizza. She popped in briefly to hug Annabelle, nibble at one of the cookies birdlike and then declare, "They're delicious Annabelle...I'm positively stuffed!" She said a quick hello to Ava and Olivia and asked where Stan was. Olivia looked solemnly and nervously at the ground when she said, "He at a business meeting, Miss Pamela."

Pamela just laughed. "Sure, Oli, what's her name?" She knew Stan Smith's character all too well. She didn't care. She was seeing someone else for coffee right now anyway.

"Well, Ciao, girlies! Keep up the Julia Child!" she said as she walked out the open back door, the same way she had come in.

Olivia cleaned up the cookie mess while Ava and Annabelle went upstairs to Annabelle's room to work. Annabelle did her homework neatly and perfectly, and rarely asked questions. Ava enjoyed her company. She was more proper and mature than most girls her age, or most girls Ava's age for that matter. She was doing better in school and was focused on her studies. Ava left and said goodbye to Annabelle. She was returning the next day and wished Annabelle a good night. The afternoon had gone smoothly, and there had been no sign of Stan Smith. She looked forward to her next meeting with Annabelle the next day.

12

"Is that your mom?" Ava asked Annabelle, on a soy-nuts-and-protein-shake snack break from a two-hour session. Ava had admired the beautiful portrait of a woman in her mid twenties wearing a tiara several times during her meetings with Annabelle, but today Ava finally felt that she had won Annabelle's confidence enough to inquire as to who Ava conjectured this beauty queen was.

Annabelle stared at the portrait for a moment as a sad look crept over her face. "Yeah," she said, sucking on her milk straw and staring at the table.

"She's very pretty," Ava said, "I see where you get your pretty face, Annabelle."

"She lives in Newport Beach now," volunteered Annabelle, still staring at the kitchen table with a melancholy gaze. Her eyes looked empty and sad, the most unhappy Ava had ever seen her.

"Was she Miss America?" Ava asked, pointing at the gleaming tiara on her head.

"Miss California," said Annabelle.

"I go to her house sometimes. She lives with Dave now and they have a boat and a new baby named Tate."

"Wow Annabelle! I didn't know you were a big sister! That's very special!"

"No it isn't," she said, finally looking up from the table.

In walked Bigshot Stan Smith with a big bag from Niketown. He was smoking a big Cohiba cigar and still wearing his Armani shades even though he was inside. He had loosened his tie and his green and blue striped collared shirt was damp with sweat.

"Everybody gets new shoes!"

As he talked on his phone, and fielded call waiting after call waiting, Ava felt like she and Annabelle were just another call waiting in a list of many, and they would "get a call right back."

He handed Ava a large silver bag from Niketown with brand new Nikes in it. He handed Annabelle three bags with six new pairs of shoes.

"Thanks, Mr. Smith," Ava said.

"OK girls, go get 'em," he said, holding up his hand to Annabelle for a high five.

She rolled her eyes, embarrassed, but gave him a cold fish high five as a consolation. He walked out of the room, whistling and carrying three more bags from Niketown.

"OK, Annabelle, take out your review sheet for the math test," Ava said.

Annabelle rolled her eyes and looked at the ground. Then she looked up at Ava with a face cuter than that ever seen on a sad puppy.

"Tutor, I hate math. It's boring. Can we go shopping at Pixie Town?" Annabelle asked.

"No, Annabelle, you have a math test, we have to go over it."

Annabelle shrugged and picked up her pencil. Ava and Annabelle started going over math, to Annabelle's dismay. Sometimes the hardest part about this job was just getting the kid to do what she was supposed to be doing. Why couldn't Annabelle concentrate? Ava was very nervous because tomorrow she had an interview with a new family. Dr. Peters had left her a message earlier in the day letting her know that there was a new family who needed a tutor, but they wanted to interview her first. Rarely did families want an interview with the tutor before employing them. This was special.

Ava and Annabelle finally finished the work. Ava said goodbye to Annabelle and walked out to her car on the street. Then she noticed something very bizarre. There was a huge black box with a pink ribbon tied around it on top of her car. Ava was excited, than nervous. What if it was a bomb?

Ava walked toward it carefully and poked it with her finger. It seemed ok, so she picked it up. She needed to use two hands it was so big. She put it on the ground and carefully undid the ribbon. She took the top off the box slowly and looked inside. She moved the bright pink tissue paper, and right there behind it, was a beautiful tan, red, and green Gucci over the shoulder bag. Ava gasped. She picked it up out of the box and put it on her shoulder. She couldn't believe this was hers. A Gucci bag this big was surely very expensive. However, she couldn't stand in the street admiring it. She had to get to her next appointment! She got in her car and drove away feeling very excited about this mystery gift. She felt around the inside of the box, trying to see if there was a card. She found one and picked it up. She slammed on her brakes as read the note:

"For you, doll. You need something to carry all that cuteness in! xoxox STAN"

Ava was shocked. However, she was more shocked at herself for actually kind of liking this.

13

The next day, Ava was feeling nervous about her job interview. The corner of Wilshire and Roxbury was busy at lunch hour. Ava saw many beautiful ladies parading to lunch. Businessmen in Italian suits talked on their cell phones as they crossed the street. Ava parked her car carefully and fumbled in her purse for change for the meter. You would think the streets were paved in gold since five minutes cost a quarter.

Ava fed the meter and then turned and walked quickly to the crosswalk at the corner. She pressed the button to cross the street and stood patiently at the light. Up walked two beautiful-looking women who were obviously together but talking to other people on their phones. They were both tall and lean. Ava thought they were probably models. The woman on the left wore a short suede skirt, black heels and a fur jacket. Her hair was long, blonde, and full of body. Her legs were tan and muscular. She gabbed away on her silver cell phone to someone who seemed like a great friend. "Oh my God, I have to show you my new Manolos!" she squealed as she bent over, put her phone right over her shoes and flashed a picture of them, right there on the corner. She flipped her head back up, pressed a couple of buttons on her phone, and tossed her long blonde hair back. She put the phone back up to her ear and squealed again, "I know, aren't they great?!?!? Unbelievable!!!"

Meanwhile, her companion stood next to her behind dark aviator sunglasses, talking away on her silver cell phone with her hand covering her mouth. She was a bit more mysterious-looking, her long brown hair slicked back in a ponytail. She was in all black clothes with dark alligator boots. She seemed to be talking about something very important.

Ava felt three feet tall next to these beautiful women. Her long blonde hair was tied back in a bun. Ava felt like her hairstyle was babyish and boring compared to their sophisticated hairdos. Ava wore a light-blue collared blouse and a gray skirt she had purchased on sale. After seeing the blonde girl's beautiful new heels, Ava noticed for the first time the scuffs on her own flat black slip-on shoes. Ava wished she had a rag to make them shinier. She felt her face looked like a little kid's, with just some powder on her skin and Vaseline on her lips. She smelled only of her boring "powder fresh" deodorant while these ladies smelled of expensive perfumes and luxurious creams. Ava's only saving grace was that she carried the brand new over-the-shoulder Gucci bag from Stan Smith. It made Ava feel like she was not completely left out. She sort of fit in. She had a clue as to what was going on. She wasn't totally lost, thanks to Stan Smith's generosity. Finally, the light turned green, Ava had to forget about feeling left out and focus on the interview she was about to have. She started to get nervous.

An "interview" was a rare request from a family. More often than not, families trusted the prestige of Educational Advantage. They didn't actually need meet the tutor first. Ava wanted to get this new job. She wanted to impress whoever they were. Ava crossed the street, focusing on these thoughts, when all of a sudden, "Love your Gucci, honey!" the tall blonde yelled to Ava, giving her a wink. Ava's face turned red, as she smiled and looked at the ground. Then she looked up at the girl and said, "Thanks," in a voice so light it was almost a whisper.

"Ciao!" the tall blonde said quickly as she continued talking into her cell phone and walking away with the best posture Ava had ever seen. Ava couldn't believe she had noticed her bag. The blonde, statuesque, designer jewelry clad bombshell had noticed Ava's bag. Ava felt like a million dollars.

Ava walked into the building's marble lobby, into the elevator, and pushed P for Penthouse.

"Hi, I'm Ava, here to meet Angelo," she said to the young beautiful woman sitting at the desk. The thin sophisticated woman did not even look up from the desk and said, "He's still in a meeting Ava, please wait on the couch." She pointed at a large black leather couch in the corner of the room, still never looking up from the desk.

Ava took a seat on the soft couch. She looked around the room at the beautiful modern artwork and stainless steel furniture. The air was on so high that Ava felt like she was freezing. She had little goose bumps on her legs. She didn't know how to sit. She crossed her legs. She crossed her arms. She didn't like that. Legs straight and together. No, not that either. Arms straight. No. She decided to read one of the magazines on the glass coffee table when a thin Asian woman dressed in a pink skirt and jacket opened the door and peeked into the waiting room.

"Ms. Fleet?"

"Yes," Ava said.

She gestured with her finger for Ava to come into the office. Ava sat down with the woman at a small stainless steel conference table. On the table were fabric samples and piles of bags. The Asian woman was very nice and extremely polite. "So, do you go to school?" she asked in the sweetest, most genuinely interested voice.

"Yes, I'm at UCLA," Ava replied.

"Oh, great!" she said happily, "I take classes at Extension but I work here so much that I don't think I'll ever have time to finish my degree," she said, laughing. "By the way, I'm Marcy."

"Hi, nice to meet you," Ava said. Marcy made Ava feel comfortable in such a nervous situation.

"So, let me tell you a little bit about the position, Ava. The family needs someone three to four days per week. Brian is shooting a film right now, so some days you would need to meet him at his trailer on set and some days you will meet them at the house on Palm Drive."

Just then, a thick Italian voice interrupted Marcy as the door swung open. "The teacher is here?" asked a tall, tan Italian man with a big round tummy.

"So sorry to keep you waiting," his deep Italian voice said as he walked in the room and took a seat at the table. He wore a perfectly pressed crisp white shirt and navy blue slacks. His gray hair was thin and brushed over his head to cover his bald spot.

"No problem," Ava said with a smile. She looked at him carefully. She knew she knew him from somewhere. She was not quite sure where.

"Hi, Angelo Martini," he said.

70

The "Angelo" Ava was sent here to meet was none other than Angelo Martini himself. She had seen his ads as she drove around town. They were usually of a scantily clad girl lying in the sand as the tide rolled over her body. Angelo Martini's name always ran along the bottom of the billboards in bright red letters. He was probably the most sought-after designer in the world. His name could be seen underneath photos of beautiful women in the hottest new dresses on the pages of *In Style*, *Glamour*, and *Harper's Bazaar*. Ava couldn't believe she was sitting right there in his office, right in front of him.

"So, miss, you can do the job or what?" he asked in his Italian accent.

Ava thought about this for a moment. A trick question?

Ava began, "Yes, I am very experienced. I work well with children-"

"Fine," Angelo Martini interrupted, "Let me show you my new season."

Angelo Martini pulled out boxes of clothes and bags from below the conference table. He held each piece up as if it were made of exotically-imported spun gold. "My handbag-the latest rage! All the girls are dying for them!" he announced as he showed Ava a handbag made of purple vinyl splattered with rainbow colored paint.

"My newest dress! All the actresses are clamoring for it. Everyone wants it for the Oscars!" he exclaimed as he showed Ava a dress made of black leather belts and steel chains. Ava thought it looked more like a dominatrix outfit than a glamorous gown for an awards show.

71

Suddenly Angelo Martini became very serious. He took a smaller item out of a black silk bag. He closed his eyes, took in a deep breath and pulled out a pink plastic chain of beads with a big gold star hanging from it. He held it up high above his head and screamed, "THE JEWELRY OF THE YEAR!!!!"

Ava watched this fashion show in awe. She smiled and made compliments about Angelo Martini's couture. "Nice, great, cool!" she said, trying to get excited about these outfits that were more fit for strippers than for fancy ladies.

Suddenly, Angelo Martini paused and asked, "So when you coming to fix my son?"

"What's best for your schedule, Mr. Martini?" Ava asked.

"OK, well we go to Italy next week. Come in two weeks, on Tuesday, at siesta," he replied.

He began to show her the way out. "Thanks for coming, little bird," he said with a big smile.

"What time is siesta?" Ava wondered to herself. Should she ask or should she know this already?

"Mr. Martini, thanks for having me. But, what time is siesta?" Ava asked and then held her breath.

"Come two, two thirty, three, four. Whenever you can make it," he replied casually. Ava was relieved.

"Oh, hey, I almost forgot. Take a little something for the road," Angelo Martini said as he handed Ava a small piece of paper. "Go to my ANGELO boutique on Rodeo Drive. I own the whole block. Pick out a little something for yourself. Any of my girls will be happy to help you," he said with a smile.

Ava looked down at the paper in her hand. She couldn't believe it when she read, "Gift certificate good for purchase at ANGELO totaling ONE THOUSAND DOLLARS."

"Thank you, Mr. Martini," Ava replied with wide eyes. One thousand dollars. Unbelievable. One thousand dollars was more money than Ava had spent on clothes the entire year.

Angelo Martini patted her on the shoulder. "Enjoy. Ciao, bella, see you soon. My son is gonna love you!" he said.

Ava walked down the long hallway to the elevator. She held the gift certificate tightly in her sweaty palm as she rode down to the ground floor, barely able to contain her excitement.

14

At 3:45, Ava rounded the corner of Melrose and joined the familiar Foundation car line. A few mothers of Annabelle's friends waved hello to Ava as she sat in the car, leaning her tired head against the window. The line was long today and Ava was sweating in her Volkswagen Cabriolet. It was at least 95 degrees and jumping into the Smiths' three-tiered swimming pool sounded much more appealing than going over math with Annabelle.

As Ava sang along to the radio, she heard a familiar cackling in the background. She turned around to see Angelica Thurman in a bright red flowy sundress hiked up to just below her behind walking toward Ago, the hottest, "it" restaurant in town, with an olive-skinned Italian man in a per-fectly-tailored navy blue suit. Angelica's long, skinny, muscu-lar, fake-tanned legs stuck out of the red dress Ava had seen at Gucci two days before. Her pedicured feet wore strappy gold sandals and they click clacked on the concrete as she walked side by side with "Renaldo." Two tall, dark haired men in black suits and sunglasses followed Renaldo and Angelica. They walked about fifteen feet behind them and spoke serious-ly into their walkie-talkies.

Angelica's long blonde hair flowed out of the floppy red hat as she excitedly discussed what seemed like a future party to be held at Ago. "So, Renaldo, I want the table on the patio, first course, the field greens with balsamic, then we've got to split the table 3 ways- enough chicken for 7, fish for 7, and veg for 7..."

Renaldo acknowledged her requests and smiled. They walked further down the street and soon were a mere three feet from Ava's car.

As Ava sat in the car, her blonde head smushed against the driver's side window, her familiar face caught Angelica's eye. Angelica stopped dead in her party-planning tracks, her heels click clacking to a halt. She bent her knees slightly, smiled what seemed like a thousand teeth, and waved so enthusiastically she could have been hailing a cab. "HIIIIIIIIIII!" she squealed at Ava, "How are you Genevieve?" Then Angelica looked at Renaldo and said, "Genevieve is the best!!! Renaldo, next time you're shopping at Saks ask for G. She is an amazing salesgirl!" and kept on walking. Renaldo gave Ava a wink and handed her his business card as Angelica turned the other way and continued her detailed explanation of the upcoming dinner party at Ago.

"Hi," Ava said with a fake smile. To Angelica Thurman it was all the same - the gal handling her mink coat and the gal handling her son's brain. She had completely mistaken Ava for a salesgirl at Saks.

Ava drove up to the Foundation, anticipating Annabelle's grand entrance into the vehicle. When Ava held up the sign, a teacher in overalls and a ponytail reached in the window and handed her a handwritten note on Smith family stationary, folded in half, with the words: **"Attn: Ava Fleet"** written on the front: Ava was slightly confused but opened the letter and read it slowly.

Dear Ava,

Today Annabelle will take a break from your lessons. We are disappointed and upset with the last meeting. We expect phenomenal professionalism from you, as we are paying a substantial fee for your services. If Annabelle says she wants to go to Pixie Town, it is expected that you drive her there and use the family credit card to charge whatever clothes, shoes, and toys she needs. Please don't let this happen again.

Sincerely,

Stan and Pamela

Ava was beyond disappointed. Her heart dropped. She thought she was hired to tutor Annabelle, not take her on a shopping trip. She felt beyond depressed. Ava felt like she lived in black and white, while the rest of the world moved on without her in Technicolor. Had she failed forever? Would the Smith family tell Educational Advantage? She had grown fond of Annabelle and looked forward to tutoring her more than any student. More importantly, Ava felt that Annabelle needed her the most. Ava wasn't sure Annabelle was so happy. Every day when Ava picked her up, she stood alone, her huge backpack hunkering over her and her brand new tennis shoes sparkling a hundred times more than her face, which always pointed toward the ground. Annabelle always stared at the floor but her eyes seemed to stare off into somewhere much further away. Ava felt that she had let Annabelle down and a feeling of sadness came over her. She felt as though she had bought tickets to a show and then shown up to hear it was cancelled. She really wanted Annabelle to do well in life; to grow up a good person. Annabelle must have been confused a little bit, with all the people coming in and out of her life. Hopefully the Smith family would call and schedule Ava again. Annabelle needed some stability in her life. Ava worried for herself and worried for Annabelle.

Ava knew she should study now that she had a free hour. However, she didn't think she would be able to concentrate. She was so upset. Maybe she would walk in the park. No, she needed a real distraction. Ava still had her gift certificate from Angelo Martini and could go shopping on Rodeo Drive until the five o'clock meeting at the Kurakis house.

15

*A*va walked into the ANGELO boutique on Rodeo Drive. Normally, she would have stuck out in this store of fancy ladies. However, today, she was cleverly camouflaged by her red, green, and beige Gucci bag from Stan Smith. "Ha, ha," she thought. She had tricked them all. She felt like she was wearing another country's military uniform and sitting in on their secret war meeting unnoticed, looking like she belonged there. Ava was not really a girl with two big Gs on her handbag, she just looked like one. She wanted to talk on her cell phone like all the rest of the ladies, but Ava had the lowest possible minutes plan, she couldn't afford to gab away while shopping. And anyways, that might make her drop something. Ava browsed for a few minutes and picked out three things right away that caught her eye. She tried them on and they made a perfect outfit. A knee length denim skirt, a cream blouse, and a pink cashmere sweater. She felt bizarre picking out these clothes. They were so expensive. Even though she wasn't paying for them she felt the guilt one feels when spending a large amount of money. Even more so, Ava wondered where she would wear these clothes. To a college party? No way, someone might spill a beer on them. To a fancy dinner? Ava was never invited to those and even if she were she would be too afraid she would spill something on them. To work? What if she accidentally got pen marks on them?

Ava brought the items up to the register and a small Asian girl looked up from the desk. Without a hello, she took the items and put them on the side of the counter. "One moment," she said, not even looking at her as she had one ear glued to her cell phone and the other leaning on the land phone and her shoulder.

Next to Ava, a busty blonde Baywatch-looking lady was arguing over some items. She looked about forty years old, but her skin did not have a wrinkle on it. Her blonde hair sat perfectly in a coif on top of her head and her ass was higher than most nineteen year olds'. Ava decided that this lady must be friends with the ladies at the Foundation Pickup Line.

"The angora sweater was purchased with a credit, the wool pants were purchased with a gift card, and the rest was on my husband's corporate charge. Just refund everything to a gift card," she explained, frustrated.

"Yes, Mrs. Valentine, I understand," said a second small Asian woman, "However, each charge must be refunded to where it was purchased."

"But I just need to purchase new items now to wear to my son's all star soccer game this weekend, so just put it all on a gift card," explained the busty blonde Baywatch mommy.

Just then a drop-dead gorgeous twenty something petite blonde who had been talking on her glittering cell phone while waiting in line behind the Baywatch mommy, moved her cell phone away from her mouth and said sternly, "I don't have a hassle like this woman. I have four things to buy and a Platinum card ready to charge them on. All of which will take one tenth of the time it will take you people to come to a solution to your drama!"

79

The small Asian salesgirl looked at the Baywatch mommy and said, "Just one moment Mrs. Valentine. Please let me make this lady's sale and I will be free to discuss your purchases at leisure."

The Baywatch mommy rolled her eyes but allowed the young, tall, petite blonde to go ahead of her while she continued gabbing on her cell phone.

The young lady was beautiful. Ava thought she looked like some of the girls in her sorority, but she was dressed in an expensive, sophisticated outfit; something no one in her sorority could possibly own. She continued to gab on her cell phone, "Yeah so I'm at ANGELO with Baldi's credit card...yeah, yeah...we were supposed to go to Miami this weekend and then he gave me some bullshit about his son's all star, all America whatever soccer game so I threw a fit and here I am...Yeah let's meet at Spago in an hour...on Baldi's Amex Platinum. OK. Bye."

The Asian salesgirl tallied up her tab and let her know that her total was $2,573.00. Without a thought, the young petite blonde placed a Platinum American Express card on the counter and tapped her red manicured acrylic nails next to it. Ava walked toward the back of the store. She had to catch her breath. Two thousand five hundred seventy three dollars!!!! That was six months of rent! Ava pretended like she was looking at some other items but continued listening to the ladies. She felt she was on a top secret mission. Ava was a military spy, camouflaged cleverly by her Gucci bag, crouching in a jungle of overpriced couture, listening intently and observing this retail war crime.

The salesgirl charged the card and then looked at the printed receipt for a moment. A little confused, she handed the young petite blonde her bag of new clothes, and said, "Thank you...Mrs. Valentine?"

The young petite blonde snapped up her bag, popped her sunglasses over her eyes, and said, "Oh, thank you honey, but I'm no Mrs. Valentine. I have no idea what she looks like."

Just then, the older Baywatch soccer mommy looked up from staring at her Gucci daily planner and stared at the young petite blonde as she walked out the door. Her eyes were like daggers as she stared at the young lady's ass swing as she walked out the front door and into the Rodeo Drive sunlight. The Baywatch mommy was furious and beyond embarrassed. The nerve of her husband.

"Yes, how can I help you now, Mrs. Valentine," the young Asian salesgirl began.

Baywatch mommy was furious. She turned around and piled her arms high with more and more items, not even checking the size or anything. She grabbed shoes, bags, everything she could get her hands on. As Ava watched the woman she was reminded of Supermarket Sweep, but this Rodeo Drive boutique was not even close to the supermarket on the game show. The woman grabbed more and more, and her face turned redder and redder. The woman finally placed the pile of things on the counter. Some items fell to the floor, as everything she grabbed could not have possibly fit on the counter.

The Asian salesgirl hustled to ring up every item. Her face too was turning red as she thought about the commission she was making. After everything had been rung up, Ava watched in horror as she saw the numbers come up on the register: $104,212.00.

The Baywatch mommy took out a Platinum card, which looked all too similar to the one the young petite blonde had paid with. She slapped it down on the counter and said, "Well, Mr. Valentine is sure doing some shopping today!"

Ava was in complete disbelief as she watched the scene. She hid behind some cashmere sweaters as the real Mrs. Valentine called her limo driver on her cell phone and explained that he needed to pull up in front and help her with "a few things." Within seconds, her driver pulled up in front and made three trips carrying all of Mrs. Valentine's purchases. Mrs. Valentine took her receipt, which was so long it looked like a family of twelve's grocery bill, and tucked it into her Chanel handbag.

After she had gone, the two Asian salesgirls talked among themselves. "Just another angry wife," said the first one.

"Why do I always get the new mistress who doesn't realize that her card has no limit?" said the second, "You made a killing today, bitch." They both laughed at each other.

Ava hesitantly took her three different items up to the register and as the second Asian salesgirl rang them up, she looked annoyed. $1,000 certainly wasn't worth her time. Without even looking at Ava, she packed the items in a bag, and then stuck out her hand. Ava handed her the gift certificate, given to her by Angelo Martini himself. As the Asian salesgirl looked over the gift certificate and spotted the Angelo Martini signature, she smiled at Ava and her face lit up.

"Lucky girl," the salesgirl said, "This is just the beginning. He's a generous one, if you're a good girl." She winked at Ava and smiled again.

"Um, thanks," Ava said nervously. She took her single bag and walked out the door. As she continued down Rodeo Drive, she thought about what the two salesgirls had said.

Being a mistress must be kind of cool if it means shopping and treating your girlfriends to lunch on your sugar daddy and his wife's platinum card. Ava got in her car and thought about the mistress and the wife in the store. She headed towards the Kurakis house. She had twenty minutes to get there.

16

$\mathcal{A}$va made the drive to the Kurakis house, which by now had become so familiar that she could almost do the drive with her eyes closed. She drove up to Kiosk number one and now passed easily through Kiosk One, then Kiosk Two, and breezed through Kiosk Three. Now that Ava had been promoted to the Kurakis' list of full-time employees, she had a magnetic pass on her dashboard, which avoided the fingerprinting and photographing she had to do before. In fact, the uniformed man at the Kiosk waved at Ava, and said, "Hello, my lady, welcome back"

Ava drove into the Kurakis driveway and saw a man standing in front waving at Ava as he watered the lawn. "Hi, Miss Ava," he said with a big smile, "How are you today?"

"Fine, thank you," Ava said.

He stuck out his hand. "Miss Ava, I'm Jonathan. I take care of things around here. Any questions, you call me," he said as he handed her his business card.

"Oh, Miss Ava, they are up in their rooms, and I know they are waiting for you. When I asked them about their homework they said, 'I don't get it.'" Jonathan laughed and shook his head. "They are smart boys but they always say they don't get it."

Ava smiled at Jonathan and walked inside the grand entrance of the Kurakis house. As she closed the door behind her she heard a screeching woman's voice yell, "Anastasia....come upstairs. I need your help!"

Ava's eyes looked up at the large grand staircase, past the large crystal chandelier and spotted Angelica Thurman with a big smile on her face, leaning over the balcony, waving hysterically at Ava. She had a fluffy red towel wrapped around her skinny body. Ava never saw her in such a natural state. She wore no makeup and her long blonde hair was in hot rollers. Her pale face and shoulders were covered in freckles. Ava never would have guessed she had so many freckles. There must have been at least a million. Angelica's bare toes hung over the edge of the balcony. They had cotton balls in between each one of them. It was unbelievable. Since Ava had always seen Angelica Thurman completely made up, she could not even fathom that an Angelica Thurman without makeup and stilettos existed. Ava was confused and skeptical. This had to be an imposter.

"An-as-stasiaaaaaa, what are you looking at??!!!" she squealed, "We have fifteen minutes!"

Ava hurried up the stairs, as her new Gucci bag from Stan Smith filled with books and a laptop, banged against her hip. When Ava reached the top of the stairs Angelica grabbed her hand and led her into her bedroom.

Angelica glanced back at Ava and said, "Nice bag. Put it down here." She pointed to a silk upholstered chaise lounge in the corner of the room as she let go of Ava's hand and ran back into the bathroom on the other side of the room. Ava put her bag down, and scanned the bedroom. It was overwhelmingly beautiful. First of all, it was about the size of or slightly bigger than the living room at Ava's sorority house. Ava could not believe she was standing in such a beautiful room. It reminded her of the palace in Versailles she saw when she went to France while backpacking across Europe after high school graduation. Everything was beautiful and detailed. The bed was the biggest bed she had ever seen. It had a puffy gold duvet and was covered in crimson and gold pillows. It looked like a huge red and gold cloud. Ava thought to herself, "If I had this room, I would never leave, because there is probably not a more beautiful or comfortable place existing in the world. "

The room contained a beautiful glass and wooden case, filled with Angelica's awards. There was an Oscar, and several others Ava had never heard of - but they were large, gold, and beautiful, and obviously very important. There were several silver picture frames, but to Ava's surprise, there were only two of Angelica with other celebrities. The frames were mostly filled with photos of Angelica and her sons; skiing, playing Frisbee, picnicking in the park, etc. Angelica may have been a bit of a scatterbrain, but she certainly loved her sons. They were more important to her than her career, although that did play a close second. In the other frames, Angelica had pictures of herself with Princess Diana, and another with John F. Kennedy, Jr. and his wife Carolyn. This case was full of precious things. Only the most important items were in there. Downstairs was a bulletin board in the kitchen filled with pictures of her at parties with all kinds of people, but this was a collection of Angelica's most prized possessions.

On the floor of Angelica's suite was a beautiful Persian rug, and the gold and red tones in the room brought out the gold and red in the rug. Then there were the windows. There were four miraculous large windows with ornate gold drapes. The windows overlooked the south side of the Kurakis property. There was an enormous lawn of the richest green color, perfectly manicured. It was so big it reminded Ava of a golf course. In the middle of this vast expanse of green was a beautiful stone fountain. It held a stone cherub in its middle who appeared to be frozen while he was dancing ballet. The cherub held a stone basket of fruit above his head and he stared up at it smiling. The water poured out from below his feet and into a large pool filled with multicolored koi fish. Beyond the grass and the fountain was the most glorious view of Los Angeles Ava had ever seen. One could see the entire city as the sun set beyond into the Pacific Ocean.

"Anastastia, which ones?!?!" Angelica asked as she gracefully emerged from the bathroom in bare feet and a drop-dead gorgeous yellow, orange, gold, and blue cocktail dress, her long flowing blonde hair cascading down her back.

Ava turned around and saw a line of eleven pairs of perfect stilettos on the floor. They stood perfectly as if they were saluting to Angelica: the Manolo Blahniks, the Guccis, the Jimmy Choos, the Pradas; all without a scuff or a scratch. They were as little children at an orphanage, on their best behavior, in their most perfect form, and their flawlessness screamed, "Pick, me! pick me, Angelica, wear me to the party! I go best with your Versace dress!"

Angelica's beautiful, brightly colored, up to her behind dress would have gone with any of them, but Ava picked a pair of gold Jimmy Choos for her.

"No, silly, you can't wear those! I'm wearing those! Which ones are you wearing?" Angelica said.

Ava just stared blankly at Angelica, "What does she mean? For me? I need a pair of shoes?....I'm going somewhere with Angelica Thurman?"

"Come on, slowpoke! We're late!" Angelica yelled.

Just then, Ava felt a tug on her denim skirt. She turned around to find little Carson staring up at her, holding a stack of lined paper. "Why are you in mommy's room? I have a math quiz tomorrow. I don't get anything, Ava."

Ava's face lit up. "Hi, Sir, how are you? Ummmm-"

"Mommy needs teacher's help tonight at the party," Angelica said, frustrated, "Carson, don't make me angry, Carmela cancelled on Mommy at the last minute and Mommy can't go to the party alone!"

"But, mama, it's so important. I don't get anything!" Carson threw his papers on the floor, frustrated and angry. "If I don't get it, I don't go to school tomorrow! I don't want to flunk! Ava you're not leaving me the day before my test! You can't!" he screamed.

Ava's heart dropped to the ground. She could feel the desperation in his eyes and the fear in his voice. To Carson, a math test was the scariest thing in the world, especially since he didn't understand any of the material. She wanted to help him, but Angelica Thurman was her boss, and she had to do what she asked, as bizarre as it seemed.

"Mr. C, I promise you'll do ok-"

"Seriously, Ava (oh my God-her real name)-we are really pushing it, pleeeeeease pick out your shoes!" Angelica screamed.

"Um, do we wear the same size, Miss Thurman?" Ava, asked, terrified, as there was no way that Ava was going to squeeze into Angelica's size zero dress and size five shoes, although the ones in the row on the floor looked more like Ava's size seven.

Carson started crying and ran out of the room, his tousled brown haired head staring at the ground. "AHHH-HHHH!" he screamed.

Ava's eyes followed him out the room. She wanted to hug him and tell him that it would be ok, he would do fine on the test, a test was not the end of the world, when Angelica interrupted, "Oh, don't worry, I called the agency and they told me what size you were, so I had Giorgio's assistant send over a few things for you!" she said, smiling, obviously proud of herself.

"I guess that was one of the questions on the application," Ava thought to herself. The application was so long, she must have forgotten that she did fill out her shoe and dress size as part of the paperwork.

"Maybe it would help to see your dress," Angelica said, proud at her bright idea,"Janelle! Bring me the Armani!"

Just then, Janelle, Angelica's personal makeup artist, emerged from the bathroom, her short brown hair tucked underneath a baseball cap. She looked like a soccer mom, in her red sweatpants and grey polo shirt and she held up a beautiful sheer black Armani dress, whose sequins glittered in the light of the crystal chandelier above Angelica's bed. Ava could not believe her eyes. The dress was long and flowy and perfect and she was going to wear it. It looked exactly like the dress she had seen Drew Barrymore wearing on the cover of Vogue this month. It was beautiful.

"It's beautiful," Ava said.

"Yeah, well, I had to get something fast. They just sent what they had out before the close of the day. They used it in some photo shoot or something," Angelica said as she walked over to her closet and started flipping through her handbags.

"Oh my God, it was the dress Drew Barrymore wore for the cover of Vogue!" Ava thought in disbelief. What a stroke of luck. This morning Ava had woken up in her sorority house in a bunk bed, and ten hours later, here she was, standing in the middle of the most elegant bedroom she had ever seen, with one of the most famous actresses in the world, and she was going somewhere great wearing a dress that was at that very moment on the cover of Vogue. It had to be a dream.

"How many more times do I have to tell you to pick out some fucking shoes?!!!??? This is my party and I must be there soooonnnn!!!" Angelica screamed.

Ava grabbed a black pair of Jimmy Choos from the stiletto lineup and raced into the bathroom. Janelle the makeup artist helped her put on the dress and, after running a brush through her hair, and patting on some quick makeup, she was ready.

Angelica was already standing smoking a cigarette in the circular driveway while Victor the limo driver arranged Pellegrino and candy in the shiny black stretch limo. Angelica patted Carson on the head as he sucked a lollipop. His mood had changed since Angelica told him he could stay home from school tomorrow. Ava walked out the front door of the house and all three of them turned to stare. The floor length Armani gown glittered in the moonlight and Ava's long blonde hair fell just above her cleavage, which was amplified by the corset in the dress. Ava

90

felt like a princess. All the clothes and shoes she was wearing were worth more than the sum of money she had made in her entire life. Ava felt she was in costume. This was not Ava, it was a girl who looked like Ava and owned these kinds of clothes and went to wherever she was about to go with Angelica Thurman.

The Armani dress was heavy from the thick black sheer fabric and the shiny crystals. Ava felt uncomfortable but tried to walk gracefully from the entryway toward the limo where Angelica and Carson were standing. The stilettos she wore were stiff and brand new. She couldn't believe these thin strappy shoes on her feet would have paid for her school books for an entire semester, and that Angelica had let her wear them. Angelica was as willing to let Ava borrow those shoes as if she were borrowing some hand lotion. It was all the same.

As Ava walked into the view of Carson and Angelica, Carson's green lollipop fell out of his mouth. "Hubba, hubba, teacher," he said, "Wow! You look different!"

Angelica squealed when she saw Ava, "OOOHH! You clean up nice, honey!"

"OK, pumpkin, Mommy will be home later!" Angelica told Carson as she patted him on the head again. Carson gave his mom a kiss on the cheek and said, "Not a sleepover, right, mommy, really coming home when it's still dark!"

Angelica smiled. As Carson stepped away from his mom, he looked up at Ava with the reddest little tomato face Ava had ever seen and he asked, "Teacher, can I kiss you goodbye too?"

"Of course, Carson, I would be honored, buddy!" Ava replied.

Ava bent her head down near Carson and stuck her cheek near his face. Then, before she knew what was going on, Carson grabbed Ava by both cheeks with his sticky little hands, turned her lips toward his, and gave her a big kiss on the lips. Then his face got even redder and he ran into the house laughing, not even bothering to tie his loose shoelaces.

As he ran away, Angelica laughed hysterically, and said, "What a charmer my boy is! I'm so proud!"

Just then she slapped Ava on the butt and said, "Come on baby, we have a party to go to!"

Victor the limo driver opened the door of the long black stretch limo and pointed inside, "Miss Ava."

"Thank you, sir," Ava replied. She got into the limo behind Angelica feeling a little more clear about what was happening. They were going to a party, at least she knew that much, and, knowing Angelica, it was going to be an interesting one.

Immediately after sitting down, Angelica pulled out her cell phone and a little fancy silk bag which she began to rummage through. She immediately started gabbing on her phone as she sucked on a lollipop.

As the limo pulled out of the Kurakis driveway, it passed through every gate and each gate opened immediately. No need to show ID, no fingerprints- they just glided through. As they passed the third kiosk, Ava rolled down her window and peeked out at the uniformed guard. He looked up at her, startled. Ava just gave him a wink as they cruised down the driveway and onto Bel Air Road.

The drive from the Kurakis house never looked as beautiful as that day. It's funny how everything looks gorgeous when you are riding in a stretch limo, wearing a dress that currently graced the cover of Vogue.

Ava passed all the beautiful homes. This time, as she saw them from the window of Angelica's limousine, Ava felt a part of the neighborhood, not a little college girl coming to work there. She suddenly felt like a woman, all grown up, going to a fancy party.

Ava gazed out the window and watched as they wound down Bel Air Road and Stone Canyon and passed the Bel Air Hotel. Angelica rolled down her window and waved to the manager as he shouted her name.

The limo wound down and out the Bel Air West Gate. Ava looked behind at the large white gates and she realized she had never been in such a grand situation in all her life. She got chills when she thought that at wherever they were going, it would get even better. The limo continued down Sunset Boulevard, and past UCLA, and made a right on Hilgard Avenue. As Ava saw the big gold UCLA letters in front of the school, she looked at the school from a different perspective. At that very moment, Ava was no longer a student there, she was an outsider. She was not a sorority girl who walked the campus every day. She was a grown-up woman just passing by. As the limo cruised down Hilgard Avenue, she spotted her best friend Evan walking with four sorority girls, most likely to the local college bar for a drink. Ava wanted to call to Evan through the window. She rolled her window down about two inches, and the five of them were within twenty feet of Ava as they crossed the crosswalk. Evan turned around and looked straight at Ava's window, curious to see who was in the limo. He saw a blonde head and squinted his eyes a little, but then grabbed one of the sorority girls on the butt and kept on walking to wherever they were going.

Ava looked over at Angelica, who kept leaning into her lap, sniffing something and then shooting her head up and wiping her nose. She sipped on champagne and talked a lot to Ava.

"I have literally spent every waking hour planning this shindig, so I hope Catcher is thankful. It was time for me to do something for him; I have been in four of his films!"

Angelica started to laugh, thinking she had said the funniest thing in the whole world. She laughed and laughed at herself, and did not stop until the limo pulled into the front of Ago. Ava saw crowds of people and photographers at the front of the restaurant. At that very moment, Ava felt she couldn't breathe and things started moving faster and faster and faster. As they waited in the valet line, Angelica squealed and jumped over right next to Ava. Angelica then reached over and rubbed Ava's leg. Ava's body was covered in goose bumps and her entire body became stiff. This was the last thing Ava had expected from Angelica Thurman, mother of Carson and Jarrod, and star of five major films.

Angelica giggled and grabbed Ava's hand. As the valet opened the limo door, Angelica and Ava walked out into the sea of paparazzi, hand in hand. A thousand flashbulbs went off in their faces. Ava felt as if wild bees were attacking. She could not get the cameras out of her face if she'd had a fly swatter. Angelica gripped Ava's hand tighter and kissed Ava on the cheek. The cameras flashed faster and faster, increasingly. "Angelica!" they screamed, "Angelica!" "Angelica!" a hundred times they screamed her name. People shoved photos of Angelica into her face and asked her to sign them. Ava looked over at Angelica, and saw her smiling and acting completely calm. She had grown used to this attention over time. Angelica and Ava got to the front of the restaurant, and Angelica posed with Ava for the last set of cameras by the door. Angelica put her arm around Ava and kissed her on the cheek again and the flash-bulbs went off faster and faster. Angelica waved at the sea of people in the entryway behind them as they walked through the doorway of the party at Ago. "Angelica! Angelica!" they all screamed again.

Ava and Angelica walked into the sea of people at the party. The music was blasting and the restaurant was decked out in white lights. The tables were decorated with white linen table-cloths and beautiful centerpieces of glass fishbowls filled with sand and shells. A few faces in the crowd turned to see Angelica walk in, but most people were eating or talking or dancing and kept on doing what they were doing. As Ava looked around the room, she recognized at least half the people from somewhere - TV or movies or magazines, she didn't remember which, but they were all familiar. Everyone was dressed impeccably in blacks, colors, glitter, pastels, everything. Angelica led Ava toward the back of the party and as they moved through the crowd, people tapped Angelica on the shoulder and gave her air kisses. Robert DeNiro kissed Angelica on the cheek as she walked by him. Tom Hanks gave her a hug and then introduced himself to Ava. Pamela Anderson smacked Angelica on the butt and then spilled her champagne, but they both laughed it off as if it were the fun-niest, cleverest, thing that had ever happened. Ava was in awe. The party was beautiful and she had never seen so many people in one place. Suddenly, she wished for a thousand eyes so she would be able to really see everything. Ava and Angelica kept walking toward the back of the party and as they passed a large table filled with people drinking and eating, Heidi Fleiss stood up and yelled Angelica's name. Angelica flashed her a wink and a smile and tossed her mane of blonde hair through her hands as she giggled, as Heidi Fleiss noticed Ava on Angelica's arm, she winked back at Angelica and said coyly, "Does your friend have a name? All I see is dollar signs!"

Ava gulped. She was in disbelief. Had Angelica been a Heidi girl?!?!....no she wasn't....or maybe that was how she met Mr. Kurakis!

Angelica just laughed and kissed Ava on the cheek again, all the while gripping her hand, like a boyfriend leading his timid girlfriend through unfamiliar territory. Ava and Angelica passed tables and tables of people, each one more exciting than the next. Arnold Schwarzenegger and Maria Shriver sat at one. Reese Witherspoon and her husband sat with a group of people at another. Hugh Hefner and six blonde Playmates sat at another.

Ava wondered excitedly which table they were going to. It had to be the best one, because it was, after all, Angelica's party. They walked back further and further, to a dark corner of the restaurant that was sectioned off by a velvet rope. A tall black bouncer stood next to the rope, and noticing Angelica, he opened the rope and let them by. As they walked in this special area, Ava noticed something peculiar: there were only women in this section. "Why would she want to be back here?" Ava thought, "The whole world is going on outside of this velvet rope." How bizarre it looked, all these dresses sitting at a table, all gabbing away and drinking as if it were the best time of their lives. Then suddenly Ava's jaw dropped. She recognized the women at the table as all well-known lesbian personalities. Heading the table was Candace Hanson, the talk show host who Ava read had just recently adopted a Chinese baby with her lover, actress Jennifer Johnson.

Next to this couple was Agnes, famous for coming out of the closet on the Oprah Winfrey Show. Sandra Ortega, pioneer of championing Latina lesbian's rights and actress on a hot new soap opera sat at the table eating an egg roll.

As Angelica and Ava walked up to the table, they all turned to stare at Ava. Each one of them looked her up and down and then, after taking it in, Sandra Ortega squealed, "Angelica! Hello! Who is your new toy?"

Angelica laughed and said, "Hi, doll, how are you? Isn't she a gem? Her name is Anastasia!"

Ava stuck out a nervous hand and uttered a small laugh, "You can call me Ava for short. Nice to meet you."

Sandra Ortega bypassed Ava's hand and instead gave her a huge bear hug and a sticky kiss on each cheek, "Hi, sugar, welcome to the club!" she said in a raspy deep voice. Ava was shaking. She was so overcome with the experiences and emotions in the last hour, her body could not take it. She saw that as she sat down, Agnes stared at Ava's shaking hand as she tried to pick up her glass of champagne. Agnes then whispered something to Jennifer Johnson, and Jennifer shook her head, and Ava swore she heard something about a "white horse" in their secret conversation.

The situation was bizarre, but it was a new experience, and Ava saw the whole thing as something she would tell Evan later. He would laugh, and she would laugh, and they would always joke about it. The women were all very welcoming, and asked Ava about her job and school, and all seemed intrigued by her very normal life. Candace Hanson asked Ava if she would tutor their Chinese baby when Tse started school and of course, Ava agreed, though that would probably not be for at least four more years. Candace told her the intricacies of their baby adoption and Ava found the whole story so touching.

Candace and Jennifer had been trying for years to adopt a baby. Finally, after thousands of dollars, and years of trying, they were able to adopt Tse. This was such a personal side of her, that Ava would never have expected based on her rough abrasive talk show attitude. Candace was a beautiful woman. She had long, rich, brown hair and a curvy body that looked amazing in her red, floor length gown. Her partner, Jennifer Johnson was equally as beautiful, though a little younger, and her demure face looked innocent pulled back in a long brown ponytail. They must have been quite a sight, the two of them, pushing baby Tse through the park in a stroller.

Ava suddenly felt comfortable at the table, as if they were all old friends, though she really did wish to be back out at the party with the fabulous room of amazing people. However, this was an experience all its own, and even though she wasn't at the heart of the party, she was enjoying herself.

While Ava had been deep in conversation with Candace Hanson, Angelica and Sandra Ortega were swapping facial stories. In the midst of discussing a controversial new type of facial lotion, Angelica put her hand on Ava's leg. Angelica moved Ava's dress to the side so her thin bejeweled hand caressed Ava's bare flesh. Ava felt Angelica's soft but bony hand, worn thin by years of partying and late nights. Ava felt uncomfortable, but did not ask Angelica to move her hand away. Ava had never had any lesbian experiences before. She knew many of her sorority sisters had experimented with it and it was almost trendy for girls her age. Ava felt so many different feelings. She did not like Angelica the way she liked boys, but tonight had made her feel something for her. She liked her in the same sense as she loved her mother or her grandmother, yet she felt the affection she had for many of her students. Angelica needed guidance. She was grown up, but immature in so many ways. Ava also felt intrigued and amazed that someone as accomplished as

98

Angelica would find Ava interesting. Ava felt her life was boring next to Angelica's glamour. Angelica was a big movie star married to a wealthy Greek shipping magnate, and Ava was barely starting out in the world. Everything was so new, and Angelica had seen it all.

Just then Angelica leaned over again, kissed Ava on the cheek, and whispered in her ear, "Thank you for coming with me, sweetie. You're beautiful."

Ava smiled at her. She felt a little uncomfortable, but she felt overwhelming affection for Angelica. She wanted to be friends with her. Ava began to feel a buzz after three glasses of champagne, so excused herself to go to the restroom. As she passed the man at the velvet rope, she felt excited to realize she would need to walk through the party again reach the restroom. She walked the longest and most roundabout way possible. Now that she was alone, men stared at her, up and down. A sexy, hunky, blonde guy she recognized from *Days of Our Lives* grabbed her arm and said, "What's a pretty girl like you doing alone at a place like this?"

"Oh, well, I just left my friends to find the restroom." Ava was nervous. He was sexy and he was talking to her! "Um, so, what's a sexy guy like you doing alone at a place like this?" Ava was shocked at her own mouth. Did that just come out? What courage a few glasses of champagne gives!

The sexy, hunky man smiled, "Good comeback, blondie....so where's your set?"

"My set of what?" Ava asked, a little embarrassed because she had no idea what he was talking about.

"Your set. Your friends."

"Oh, we're in the back at that big table," Ava said as she pointed to the roped off area where she had been sitting.

Sexy hunky soap opera man looked at the table in the distance, and then looked at Ava as if she were an alien.

"You're back there, with them? I would have never thought...ummm....ok." He shook his head and looked a little disappointed.

"Well, um, cool, too bad, ok." He tapped Ava on the shoulder, "See ya later blondie..."

Just like that, he walked away. Ava had made it out of the Estrogen Table and then blown it with the soap opera hunk. She was disappointed, but still couldn't get over how excited she was to be at the party. She would tell her sorority sisters, who were all probably at Moloney's tonight, and they would not believe it was true.

Ava walked through the party, bumping every second into someone exciting. She got to the bathroom and splashed her face with some water. She looked at herself in the mirror and wanted to remember this forever. Hopefully she would be able to get one of those pictures from the paparazzi outside. This was an exciting evening, very different from the majority she spent at the library or at the University Center.

Ava walked out the bathroom and back through the party. It was dying down and people were leaving. She walked back to her table and the bouncer smiled as he let Ava past the velvet rope.

At this point, Angelica was very drunk, was hitting the table and laughing. A few of the ladies had left, and the table was quieter and smaller.

"Hey doll, where have you been?!?!" Angelica squealed as she noticed Ava.

"I think its time for bed, babe," Angelica said. "Will you call the driver and tell him we're ready?" Ava wanted to call him, but, of course, Ava did not know the number of the driver. Ava took Angelica's cell phone and scrolled through her phone book past Bonaducci, Bush, Carnegie, DeNiro...ah ha Driver!

Ava dialed the number.

"Oh, hi sir, this is Ava, Angelica is ready to be picked up now."

"Yes, miss," he answered in his Spanish accent. "Out front two shakes of a lamb's tail."

"Thank you, sir," she said.

"So polite you are, miss."

Angelica was hugging everyone goodbye, stumbling a bit, and brushing the hair away from her big smiley face as Ava held her hand and escorted her out the door.

Ava smiled and waved back at the table, "So nice to meet you! Goodnight!"

Jennifer Johnson smiled behind her cigarette and said, "Bye babe, call me!"

Agnes waved and said the same, "Yeah babe, get my number from Angie!"

Angelica and Ava walked out to the front of the restaurant where there were plenty of paparazzi waiting, this time with video cameras, too. Ava and Angelica walked to the limo and Victor the limo driver, of course, had the door open, waiting for them. Cameras flashed and followed them all the way into the limo. They settled in the back seat, Angelica kicked off her heels and yelled to Victor, "Jack in the Box, please!"

Victor pulled slowly out of the driveway and pulled onto Melrose. Angelica kicked off her shoes. Within a few minutes, they were at Jack in the Box, in the drive-through line. Angelica rolled down her window and her glazed eyes looked over the menu.

"Welcome to Jack in the Box. Can I take your order?" the speaker shouted.

"Yes, hi, one chicken fajita pita, large curly fries, cappuccino shake, and onion rings," Angelica said.

"Anything for you babe?" Angelica asked Ava in a drunken slobbery voice.

"Um, I'll just have a water,"Ava said.

"Water, no!" Angelica shouted.

She leaned back into the speaker and, "One more order of fries please," she said. The speaker read back the order and gave the total,"$12.72."

The limo pulled forward and Angelica excitedly grabbed her greasy bag of fried food and handed the cashier a ten and a five, and the limo sped off. As the limo pulled away, Angelica munched happily on her French fries and reviewed the party with Ava. "Sandra's dress was horrible. I have one hundred bucks on that she gets railed by Joan Rivers for her horrible outfit," Angelica declared as she sipped her shake. "MMM, Jack in the Box is the bomb! Ha ha ha! 'The bomb' what my kids always say," Angelica smiled.

Ava could not believe Angelica bypassed the caviar and champagne at her own party, that she had paid for herself and instead picked up a $12.00 dinner for two at a drive-through Jack-in-the-Box. She was really just a down home girl. It seemed the glitz and glamour were sometimes just part of Angelica's act. Ava felt more comfortable around Angelica when she acted this way. Ava did not feel as intimidated. They were friends.

The limo wound around Sunset Boulevard and up Bel Air Road. Angelica licked her greasy fingers as her eyes began to close. Before they had reached the house, Angelica had nodded off. Her beautiful dress was soaked with grease from the paper bag from Jack in the Box and her head bobbed against the window. The limo pulled up slowly into the circular driveway and came to a stop.

Victor opened the door on Angelica's side, picked her up like a little baby and carried her in the house. Her limp body hung over his arms as he walked up the grand staircase and put her gently to bed. Ava followed them, carrying Angelica's shoes and handbag behind her up the stairs. Ava was tired and felt tipsy from all the drinking. She followed Victor into Angelica's room, and put the shoes and handbag on the floor next to Angelica's bed.

Angelica didn't make a peep as Victor pulled down her covers and tucked her in bed. She looked comfortable, even though she was still wearing her dress and all her makeup. Ava and Victor left the room and closed the door slowly. They tiptoed slowly down the stairs and were almost to the bottom when they heard Angelica's door open. Ava turned around and saw a small figure opening the door, holding a teddy bear. The figure turned around, too. Upon seeing Ava, it dropped its teddy bear and ran over to her. When he came into the light, Ava saw a pajama-clad Carson with a big smile on his face. He jumped up and gave her a big hug.

"Are you sleeping over teacher? I have an extra bed in my room! You can sleep there!"

"No, buddy, I need to go home to my own house, but thank you for inviting me!" Ava said, as she brushed his hair through her hands. "I will see you tomorrow, right?"

"Yep," he said. "Do you wanna play legos for a little bit, even though you can't sleep over?" Carson pleaded with her.

"I wish I could, Carson, but I have school tomorrow, and I'm so tired," Ava said.

"OK, Ava, I have school, too, and I am tired, too," he said. "He jumped out of her arms and picked up his teddy bear. "I'm going to sleep with mommy then!" he said.

Victor the driver snapped, "Mami is sick, boy, get to your room."

Carson frowned and looked at Victor. He stuck his tongue out and ran back in his room. Victor mumbled something to himself as he and Ava continued down the stairs. Victor turned around and said to Ava, "Miss, I'll drive you home, you drink lots of champagne, yes?"

Ava thought about this for a moment.   "Well, but my car is here."

"OK, miss, I pick you up tomorrow afternoon before you come over again, and you get your car then?" Victor suggested.

"OK, thank you Victor," Ava said.

Ava stopped to use the restroom as Victor walked outside and started the limo. As she washed her hands, she looked at herself in the beautiful dress and smiled. The evening had been beyond amazing. She walked out and started making her way towards the door when she heard a whisper come from above her.

"Sweet dreams, pretty."

She looked behind her to see Jarrod leaning over the banister in nothing but boxer shorts and his ripped athletic chest. Her heart beat quickly.

"Thanks," she whispered and smiled as her stomach filled with butterflies.

He blew her a kiss and watched her walk out to the limo. Ava got back in the limo, and carefully took off Angelica's Jimmy Choos. Ava was so tired after the long night, she lay down across the back seat of the limo as Victor drove her home and she thought of Jarrod. She wished he was in the car with her at that very moment.

Before she knew it, Victor had pulled into the driveway of her sorority house, and was tapping her on the head, "Wake up, miss, you home now," he said.

Ava sat up and got out of the limo. "Thank you, sir," Ava said.

Ava yawned and walked up the stairs to her sorority house. She held up the train of the beautiful Armani dress as she walked. A few girls sitting in the living room stared at her as she walked past them and up to her room. As she carefully took off the beautiful dress and hung it on her best wooden hanger, she giggled to herself and thought of Jarrod Kurakis. She felt the carriage had turned back into a pumpkin-but not really. Actually, it was coming back tomorrow afternoon to pick her up! What a wonderful magical night it had been!

17

Ava awoke slowly on Friday morning. She felt she could have slept all day. She yawned as she made her bed, showered, dressed, and then went downstairs to make a cup of coffee. No one else was awake at this time. She was the only girl in all of the Kappa Kappa Gamma sorority who had an 8:00 am class on Friday. She liked being alone in the morning. She could read *The New York Times* and drink her coffee alone. The silence was a nice way to start off the day.

After finishing her coffee, Ava grabbed her backpack and double-checked to make sure she had all the books she needed for the day. At 7:40 she walked out the front door and headed over to her class. She went over Shakespeare in her head and made imaginary charts of all the information she needed to know.

She walked into her class and took a seat at the front. The midterms were handed out and she finished hers quickly-in half an hour. She handed in her midterm and decided to head over to the library for some studying. The library was empty at this time, but Ava sat for an hour and read over her notes for her Milton lecture so she would be prepared for the quiz. It was now almost 10:00 and Ava needed to head over to the south side of campus. She had not spoken a word since the night before, and she felt she needed to get back to society. She walked out the front door of the library and down the steps.

Ava noticed Amy Gellar and Jenna Smith from her sorority sitting on the front steps of the library with one other girl she did not recognize. Ava was happy to see familiar faces. They were all huddled around the latest issue of *The Nationwide Examiner.*

"Hi," Ava said. They were the first words she had said in hours. "What are you guys looking at?"

All three looked up from the magazine, stared blankly at Ava and said nothing.

"Hello?" Ava said, confused.

"Nice," declared Amy Gellar as she stuck out the front cover of the magazine for Ava to see.

Ava gasped. There in the corner of the front page, clear as crystal, was a photo of Angelica Thurman kissing Ava's cheek. The headline screamed, "Angelica's Hot Young Thing!" Ava couldn't believe her eyes. She grabbed the magazine out of Amy's hand.

"So, who did you meet? Is she your girlfriend now? Are you engaged?" The unidentified girl asked a million questions nonstop.

Jenna Smith slapped the girl's arm.

She hoped that this would not cost her her important job at Educational Advantage. What if they saw it? Hopefully, this would not jeopardize her employment. That was the most important thing. As Ava stared at the picture, she suddenly felt flashbulbs go off in her face again. She looked up to see a lone man dressed in black, firing off his camera.

"Hey, baby, where you and your lady going tonight? Where's the hot spot baby?" the photographer asked in his thick Middle-Eastern accent as he fired more and more shots.

Ava didn't know what to do, so she smiled at them and then turned around. "Bye guys," she said to her sorority sisters and their friend as she walked quickly away.

"Hey, give us back the magazine," they said as Ava pretended not to hear them. Ava felt the paparazzo follow her. He was going to come to class with her! More flashbulbs followed and more questions.

"Is Angie gonna pick you up from school, baby? Is Angie gonna bring you your lunch, baby? Do the kids like mommy's new girlfriend?"

Ava stopped and turned around and spoke sternly to the photographer, "Leave them out of this. Stop following me and leave them alone."

Ava continued walking to class. She had an important quiz. This silly mess was not going to make her perform badly on a quiz she had spent hours studying for. She walked into the restroom. Thankfully, it was illegal for the male photographer to follow her in there. Double-thankfully, the bathroom was empty.

Ava looked at herself in the mirror and put her copy of *The Nationwide Examiner* away in her backpack. She took her rubber band out of her hair and pulled her ponytail down.

She ran her fingers through her long blonde hair and put it back up again neatly. She splashed some water on her face, and reapplied her lipstick. She took a deep breath and was ready to go to class. She walked towards the exit. Thank goodness the man was gone.

Ava walked into her classroom and took a seat in the back. She pulled the hood of her sweatshirt over her head and went unnoticed as she took her quiz.

Ava came home at 2:00 pm from her classes. She walked through the doorway and saw the voice mail light blinking on her phone. She pressed play in the machine and was shocked to hear that in the few hours she had been gone there were "Forty three new messages." Ava listened intently and grabbed a pen. Normally, she needed a pen in case there were messages for Bobbi she needed to write down. However, today, they were almost all for her.

"Hi, Miss Fleet, this is Stasia from the Gay and Lesbian Alliance. We wanted to discuss you having your own float in this year's Gay and Lesbian parade..."

beep

"Hi, this message is for Ava Fleet, this is Garreth from *The London Enquirer*. Wanted to set up a short phone interview if possible..."

beep

The next forty messages were all of the same nature save for a few messages for Bobbi and another from the Kurakis household itself, having nothing whatsoever to do with the events that transpired this morning.

"Wednesday 1:43 pm: Hi, Miss Ava, it's Jonathan from the Kurakis house. Angelica has asked that you meet her, Carson, and Jarrod at the Beverly Hills Library today. The men are here working on the gazebo and the noise is just too much. "AHHHHH!" Angelica screamed in the background. Anyway, gotta go, see you at the library at 4:00. Victor will pick you up in the limo at 3:30 and Angelica, the boys, and I will see you there at 4:00. Thank you, Miss Ava."

Ava thought it was unusual that even after her night out with Angelica, Jonathan still called her. Why didn't Angelica call Ava herself? Weren't they friends now? She thought they got along so well at the party.

As she put on her sweater she thought about how bizarre it was that Jonathan called her. Did Angelica not have time to call her? Was she too busy? She thought their relationship was different now. Maybe she was mistaken. She walked downstairs to see what was for lunch at the Kappa Kappa Gamma house today. She got in the lunch line and as she made a salad with chicken and Italian dressing, she listened to the other girls as they talked about the fraternity party the night before. Ava wanted to chat, but she had nothing to say because she hadn't gone with them. Some people stared at her and whispered, mostly younger girls who didn't know Ava. Thankfully, nobody asked her about *The Nationwide Examiner*. Ava sat at a table alone and read *The LA Times*. She liked to read her horoscope and "Dear Abby." She occasionally felt the stare and heard the whisper of a sorority sister...."I've heard of dating an older guy, but an older girl?"..."That's why she always says she is going to the library. It's her alibi." Ava just ignored them and continued eating.

Ava finished her lunch, then washed and dried her salad bowl. She headed back upstairs. As she walked past the living room, she saw at least thirty of her sorority sisters with their faces pressed up against the large bay window facing the front of the sorority house looking out into the street. Their backs were all to Ava as she peeped her head in to see why they were all staring out the front window. She couldn't see a thing over all their heads.

They whispered among themselves. "I bet it's for Julia Daniels from Delta Gamma next door. I heard she was dating a pro football player," suggested Amy Gellar, recording secretary of Kappa.

"I heard they broke up," said Bobbi Francis, always the all-knowing gossiper.

"What are you guys talking about?" asked Ava.

"Look! Who's it for?" Bobbi said as she pointed outside to the street. Ava looked over and was able to see what they were all talking about. Parked in front of the house was Angelica Thurman's black stretch limo. In front of it stood Victor, dressed in his formal black suit with the regal Kurakis family emblem over the front pocket.

"Oh. They're already here," said Ava as she waved at Victor through the window.

As Ava turned around and walked quickly upstairs to get her things, all thirty sorority sisters turned to stare at her.

"Excuse me?!?!" asked Jenna Smith, "That limo is for our very own Ava Fleet? Does it belong to that actress she's dating?"

"Um, Bobbi, you're her roommate. Please explain," insisted Amy, as she smacked Jenna Smith on the head and she squealed and fell to the ground.

"I have no clue," replied Bobbi blankly.

Suddenly Ava emerged at the bottom of the staircase carrying her large Gucci bag from Stan Smith. She headed towards the front door when Bobbi stopped her dead in her tracks.

"Um, what's going on here? Gucci bag? Limo? Girlfriend?!?! Excuse me, Posh Spice, but what have you done with my roommate?" Bobbi asked Ava sternly.

Ava smiled at her. "It's not my limo, silly. My job had to pick me up in their limo today, that's all," said Ava.

"I so don't get it. I expect there will be some explaining later," said Bobbi.

"Of course, I'll tell you all about it," said Ava.

Ava walked down the front stairs to the limo, where Victor opened the door for her. She settled into her seat, rolled down her window and waved back at all her sorority sisters who were waving hysterically at her and blowing kisses.

Victor dropped Ava off at the Beverly Hills library early. He had to go down the block to pick up Jonathan, Angelica, Carson, and Jarrod who were shopping in Beverly Hills.

Ava walked in through the front door of the two-story brick building. To her surprise, at first glance, the Beverly Hills library was more normal a library than she had expected. There were hundreds of books, and an area with tables and chairs. However, she noticed that the furniture was much nicer than in many other libraries she frequented. The books were also arranged differently. The first thing she approached was an ornate display of romance novels. Hovering near the display were many glamorous Beverly Hills ladies carrying expensive handbags and wearing bejeweled Jimmy Choos and Manolo Blahniks. They stood in silence, each engulfed in their respective Jackie Collins or Danielle Steel novel. She recognized some ladies from The Pickup Line at the Foundation. They all read intensely as they waited for their children to be done with their one-on-one reading tutors.

Ava walked quietly past them and into the magazine area. There were hundreds of magazines in plastic covers on the wooden shelves. She couldn't believe her eyes. The Beverly Hills library carried the latest issues of every possible magazine one could imagine. Ava would never need to buy a magazine again! Here they were for free!

Ava found so much of Beverly Hills a bizarre paradox. Why were so many things free in one of the wealthiest cities in the world? There is an overstock of parking lots on Rodeo Drive with signs screaming "TWO HOURS FREE!" Angelica Thurman, who could easily afford her own shopping expeditions, was always talking about her free stuff; a free Rolls Royce for the weekend from Beverly Hills Rolls Royce to "see if she liked it," gift bags full of free clothes, cell phones, and gym memberships every time she went to a party, or free ten-pound bags of coffee from the Coffee Bean so the Kurakis family could determine if they would like to serve it at their many dinner parties or stock it on their private plane. And now, in the Beverly Hills library, Ava had discovered the free magazines!

Sometimes on the weekends, Ava would use her lunch money to buy two or three fancy fashion magazines. It was a big sacrifice but she loved doing it. She read each page carefully. Now she would come here and read them for free. Unbelievable. Several fancy ladies and stylish gentlemen sat at the tables reading *Vogue, Glamour, Harper's Bazaar, Vanity Fair, People, US, Star,* and oh no...*The Nationwide Examiner.* Ava walked by them, and some people looked up at her, but nobody blinked an eye. Angelica Thurman's hot date for a night was no big deal to these people. There were even some faces right there at the library that Ava recognized as possibly as famous as Angelica Thurman herself. Ava noticed that the two or three soap and reality TV stars were actually too busy reading articles about themselves to even notice or care about her. Ava felt relieved. Like all hot gossip in Los Angeles, her story had been replaced by something more interesting and/or controversial within a few hours.

Ava walked to the back of the library to find a wonderful children's books area. Ava was envious. She wished she had had such a candy store of literature when she was little. There were hundreds of picture books, fairy tales and expensive paintings of *The Cat in the Hat* and *Peter Pan* on the walls. A little boy wearing brown Gucci loafers sat on a puffy red couch reading *Green Eggs* and *Ham* aloud to a small girl with blonde pigtails wearing a pink Christian Dior backpack.

Ava left the children's section and noticed a huge media area with videos and DVDs. They had so many wonderful things! You could rent a DVD for free! She couldn't believe this. The UCLA library also had a nice selection of DVDs, but this was like being in Blockbuster itself. All the DVDs looked brand new. There was even a movie Ava had seen in the theater not that long ago. Ava felt that discovering the Beverly Hills library was the equivalent of striking gold in her own backyard.

Ava went to the travel book section and pored through guides about faraway places she hoped to visit one day. She looked through books on Bali and Singapore. What enchanting places! She picked up a book on Italy and flipped through the colorful pages. How beautiful this country looked. Ava hoped one day to travel the world, see all the miraculous places, and meet all the interesting people. Ava looked at her watch and saw that it was 5 minutes to 4:00. She walked upstairs and sat at a table with four chairs. She began getting out her pencils and waited for the Kurakis family to arrive.

The dead silence abruptly broke and heads turned when Angelica Thurman marched into the Beverly Hills library, talking on her Swarovski crystal-covered cell phone and carrying four ice blended mochas from the Coffee Bean on a paper tray. She was flanked by Jonathan and her two boys, who all walked like soldiers right in a row behind her. She wore a short red cocktail dress and tall clear stiletto pumps. Her blonde hair was in a big fancy up-do. Her chunky diamond jewelry made her seem larger than life. Even though there were plenty of fancy ladies in the library, Angelica still stuck out like a sore thumb. Ava thought Angelica couldn't possibly, actually, really be there in the library. Someone must have used Photoshop to cut Angelica out of *Vogue* and paste her into the second floor of the Beverly Hills library. She spotted Ava, waved at her hysterically with her cell phone hand, and smiled.

"OK, bye, doll," she said into her cell phone and snapped it shut. Angelica spoke in her normal loud voice, not a whisper like everyone else in the library. "Hi, babe," she said as she handed Ava an ice blended mocha, took a seat next to her and started sipping on her own coffee drink.

115

"Hello," Ava said, "Thank you so much for the coffee."

"Yeah, babe," Angelica said nonchalantly as she looked around the library. "Who is their decorator? This place is horrible. I'm going to have to have a word with whoever the General Manager at this place is."

Angelica then turned her attention to Ava and her two boys, who were now sitting quietly together at the table, with their books out, ready to work.

"OK guys," she said, "I'm going to wait at one of those tables at the other end. You guys do your thing."

"Bye mommy," said Carson.

"See ya mom," said Jarrod.

Angelica stood up quickly and walked grandly toward the other end of the library. She sat at another table and looked around the library. It appeared she was going to be quite bored for the next hour as she tapped her fingers on the table. Suddenly, Angelica's eyes lit up as she noticed something on a nearby shelf. She hopped up and ran over to the bookshelf. She let out a yelp as she saw a book that excited her. Ava looked over at her and saw Angelica grab a large thin children's coloring book titled, *You Can Draw Fashion Models*!

Angelica, her cell phone, her diamonds, and her new coloring book, *You Can Draw Fashion Models*! took a seat at a nearby table.

"Jonathan, I need some crayons," she said matter-of-factly.

"Yes, Ms. Thurman, right away," he replied as he walked off.

Ava, Carson, and Jarrod sat at the table and began doing their work. Ava mainly worked with Carson as Jarrod did his own studying for History. As she worked with Carson, several thoughts ran through her head. Why did Angelica treat her this way? They had spent an entire evening together and at this very moment, they were featured together on the cover of *The Nationwide Examiner*. Maybe Angelica hadn't even seen *The Nationwide Examiner*. Maybe it meant nothing to her, as she had been on hundreds of magazine covers. Ava felt sad and rejected. She thought they had hit it off. She had actually enjoyed her time with Angelica, and experienced the greatest night of her life that night. Maybe Angelica didn't care. Ava had just been another publicity stunt. Ava felt used - more than she ever had. She remembered once in high school when a boy had kissed her just to make his ex-girlfriend jealous. That felt bad, but this felt worse.

The sadness filled her heart, but she needed to help Carson with his work. "Okay, I don't get number four," Carson began.

Ava began explaining Carson's work to him when she felt something rubbing her calf. Startled, she repeated her instructions to Carson. "You just said that!' he squealed, laughing. Ava continued and realized it was Jarrod rubbing his foot on her leg. Ava got butterflies in her stomach. As Carson attempted his next problem himself, Ava looked over at Jarrod. He winked at her. She winked back. She loved it.

"Check my answer, tutor!" Carson said.

117

Ava looked down at his paper. "Good job, buddy!"

He ran over to show his mom and Ava was left alone with Jarrod. Angelica looked up at Carson, squealed, and gave him a hug.

"You're a genius, babe!" she yelled, as the whole library turned again to stare at this woman who had blatant disregard for the "Silence" signs posted throughout the Beverly Hills library.

Ava and Jarrod hadn't even heard her. They just stared at each other. Silence had never spoken so many words at one time. Ava smiled nervously and Jarrod made words with his mouth: "Can I call you tonight?" he said with no sound as he made a phone with his hand. Ava smiled back nervously.

"Yes!" she whispered on the outside to Jarrod. "YES!" she screamed on the inside as her heart beat quickly.

Carson interrupted them after he had shared with his mom. Angelica continued drinking her ice blended mocha and drawing fashion models with the crayons Jonathan had purchased at Rite Aid drug store down the street. Several people noticed her and whispered. Two young men walked up to her and asked her for her autograph.

Ava continued with her two students. The boys were doing well. They were improving. Ava was so proud of them. She couldn't stop thinking about her upcoming phone call from Jarrod.

18

*A*va returned to Educational Advantage for her first evaluation. She walked into the office on Westwood Blvd. Ava felt comfortable in this place that at one time felt so intimidating.

The happy receptionist greeted her warmly. Dr. Peters appeared at the door and smiled, "Nice to see you, Ava. How have things been going?" he asked.

"Everything is going pretty well," she said, as he led her down the long hallway she remembered from her interview and first meeting.

"Great," he said. "We'll meet in the conference room again. Can I get you anything? Coffee? Juice? Water?" he asked.

"Oh, yes, some water please," Ava replied.

Dr. Peters sat Ava down at the large oak table.

"Just a minute, I'll be back with your water," he said.

"Thanks," Ava said.

After he left, Ava looked around the room. She was so nervous the first time she had been here, she barely noticed the lovely painting of the ocean on the wall. Ava thought about how far she had come since being in this room, only one month ago. Back then, she was a nervous little girl, full of hope of getting a part time job. Little did she know, she would meet such interesting people: Annabelle, Little Z, The Kurakis family, and Angelo Martini. So much had happened in a month. She had had so many interesting experiences, and who knew what else was coming?

Dr. Peters walked in the doorway carrying a glass of water for Ava and a large folder filled with papers. He sat down and smiled. "Well, Ava I have good news which means this meeting will be very short," he said as he began rummaging through his folder of papers. "Your overall feedback from the parents is very positive. Let's start with Zeus Johnson."

"Oh, yes, Little Z. I've never met his parents."

"Right. They observe your meetings via web cam," said Dr. Peters nonchalantly.

"Oh, ok," said Ava, surprised. Ava was shocked. She had no idea she was being observed.

"Yes, they're normally with their trainer during your scheduled meetings with Little Z so they just run on the treadmill and watch the whole thing in their gym," Dr. Peters said with a smile.

"OK," said Ava. She thought this was very bizarre. Why didn't they just come downstairs and meet her in person?

Dr. Peters, sensing Ava's uneasiness, asked matter-of-factly, "You do remember the release form you signed when you commenced employment at Educational Advantage, correct?"

"I guess so," Ava replied as Dr. Peters produced the form authorizing any and all parents to videotape, tape record, or photograph any of the tutoring sessions. Ava had been so nervous when she went for the first meeting, she had barely remembered it, but there was her signature on the dotted line, clear as crystal.

"Anyway, they're very pleased with your work. They applaud your tying-in Tupac to Little Z's poetry studies. No negative feedback whatsoever here," declared Dr. Peters.

Ava was happy. She didn't know Little Z even had parents but she was pleased that they liked her.

"Next, Jarrod and Carson Kurakis. Jonathan filled out the feedback forms. It seems things have been going well with this family as well. They are very satisfied with your services and the only comment they have is that you shift the focus of Jarrod's lessons to solely preparing for the SATs, as they are satisfied with his progress in his academic subjects," said Dr. Peters.

Ava was pleased with their feedback as well. Ava wondered if Dr. Peters had seen the photo in *The Nationwide Examiner*. If he did, he wasn't saying anything about it. However, he probably didn't read those magazines. He looked like he stuck to *The Wall Street* Journal and *Time Magazine*. Actually, he probably didn't know that Angelica Thurman was the mother of the Kurakis boys anyway.

"OK, moving right along..." Dr. Peters began as a frown came across his face.

"Oh no," thought Ava. Someone had made a bad comment. "What have I done wrong?" she thought. An almost perfect review, except for...

"Pamela, Annabelle's - er, guardian, I guess, I'm not so sure myself..." Dr. Peters began. "Her comments read, 'Does not adjust well to unique requests.'"

"Sorry about that, Dr. Peters," Ava said.

"Well, Ava, what happened here?" Dr. Peters asked, concerned.

"Well, Annabelle asked me to take her shopping and I told her that we needed to focus on her schoolwork."

"Ah," said Dr. Peters, "Sounds like a misunderstanding. However, perhaps you should find a less abrasive way to talk to Annabelle."

"What?" Ava thought, "This was my fault? A child asks me to take her shopping when I am supposed to be tutoring her and I was TOO ABRASIVE???!!!"

"Yes, Dr. Peters. Of course. I'll do a better job," Ava replied.

"OK, well, let's not have any more problems okay?" Dr. Peters asked. "Overall, your reviews from other families are good, so I assume this is just a bad match. Sometimes certain families just don't get along with certain tutors. They just don't fit. It's nobody's fault. Anyway, the Smith family thinks Annabelle will work better with a male tutor, so I am going to place someone else with them."

Ava nodded her head, "Yes, of course, no more problems." She felt so sad inside. She did her best to hold in the tears. Pamela had seemed so friendly. Ava thought Pamela liked her. Maybe she had found out about Stan Smith's gifts and wanted Ava out of the house. Ava was going to miss Annabelle. They were friends now and Ava knew inside that Annabelle would be sad to see her go.

"OK, now moving right along. The good news is that Mr. Martini was impressed with you at the interview and is ready to start. Good job." Dr. Peters said.

"Based on your overall positive review, I think you're ready for two more students, if your schedule will allow it," Dr. Peters said.

"OK," said Ava, excited about who she would be getting next.

"Well, these assignments are a little more challenging," began Dr. Peters, "First we have the Taft family. Their daughter Vanessa is doing horribly in school, three Cs and two Fs. The parents are baffled as to why. She goes to a strict French school and there have been no apparent problems at school as reported by Vanessa's teachers," explained Dr. Peters.

"Your next student is Nora Zhirhanian. She is doing fine in school, except for English class. Her reading and writing are not strong; her parents want you to work on basic language arts skills with her so that her grade can come up from a C-."

"OK," said Ava. She was happy that Dr. Peters was trusting her with cases that were a bit more challenging than the first three.

Dr. Peters handed her a piece of paper. "Here is their contact information. Give them both a call tonight and set things up," he said as he showed Ava out the front door. "Good job, Ava. You make Educational Advantage proud."

As Ava walked to her car, she felt mixed emotions. She was happy that her evaluation was good overall. She had done a good job with Little Z, the Kurakis family, and Mr. Martini. However, she was very disappointed with the Smith family. She thought they liked her. Ava thought Pamela Smith was the most perfect-looking woman she had ever seen. Why didn't she like her back? Ava felt that Annabelle was a lost soul and she would only get worse and more confused if people kept coming in and out of her life like as they had been for the last eleven years. This was a much bigger job than Ava had expected to take on. She was now involved in these students' everyday lives. She had become part of their routine, and Ava knew it was hard on a child to change their routine. She would simply do her best. She suddenly felt she not only had to take care of herself and do well at UCLA, but now she had responsibility to these children. It was a challenging but welcome responsibility for Ava. She truly wanted to do a good job.

19

Ava drove slowly up Benedict Canyon. She looked carefully at the addresses painted on the curb...1800, 1810, 1812...ah ha 1814. Ava's eyes moved slowly up from the street to the house whose number matched. As her eyes met the monstrosity before her, her mouth gaped open. She had driven on this street before, and always wondered who lived inside houses so big. Some of them looked like the White House, and others looked like they were so big you could not possibly see every room in one day...or even use all of them in a lifetime. The gigantic palace in front of her was just that. It sat proudly behind a gate of gold. It was big, white, and towering. Pillars lined the front of this home and the sound of a waterfall provided background noise. The windows were lined with gold trim. The front door was so big it looked to be designed to allow a horse and carriage to enter. Ava pulled up to the golden gate and rang the doorbell. She looked up to see a security camera rotating around to point directly at her head. There was a buzz and slowly the grand gates opened. Ava parked her car in the driveway and walked up four marble stairs to get to the monstrous entrance. She tried to lift up the huge golden knocker but it was too heavy. She put down her Gucci bag from Stan Smith and used two hands to lift up the knocker and slam it down. She grunted as she flew backward. The door opened slowly and a tiny, skinny girl opened the door. She looked like an ant in this gigantic doorway. Her hair was long and black and her fuzzy pink pajamas and slippers all matched. She smiled a big smile as she said shyly, "Hi, I'm Nora." Her face turned rosy pink.

Ava smiled back, "Hi, I'm Ava."

"Do you like chicken?" she asked.

Surprised, Ava replied slowly, "…Sure I do." Ava was a little confused but went along with the shy little girl's question.

"We've been waiting for you," she said.

Ava walked inside to see that it was even grander than the outside. Ornate Persian rugs lined the floor. A gigantic crystal chandelier hung from the middle of the entryway. The furniture was detailed and screamed out with bright reds, blues, and oranges. However, Ava found it odd that this luxurious furniture was lined with plastic.

The little girl led Ava back into the house. As she entered the kitchen, the most delicious aroma of Persian cooking filled her nose. Standing over a steaming pot of something delicious stood a plump Persian woman in a long red dress. She looked up at Ava and a huge smile crept across her face. "Hello, thanks so much for coming. We've been waiting for you," she said, her thick Persian accent echoing in the large kitchen.

She leaned over the stove and pressed an intercom button and yelled something in Farsi. Suddenly, Ava heard footsteps coming down the grand staircase behind her. The man of the house and his other son and daughter emerged. They all smiled and welcomed Ava.

Ava sat down to eat with the entire family. She did willingly, as she was very hungry. She was however, a little confused. They did know that they were paying her for her time the minute she walked in the door. The agency had explained that. So why did they want Ava to eat with them? Most families didn't want to waste a minute once Ava walked in the door. They wanted to get right down to work. It was nice that this family was inviting Ava to eat with them. She just hoped they understood that they were paying her to do that. They seemed so nice, Ava would have come for free, but today she was scheduled to tutor Nora and then in one hour, she had to get to her other new student, Vanessa Taft.

"So, you go to UCLA?" the mother asked excitedly as she passed Ava a large bowl of green rice.

"Yes, I am studying English," replied Ava.

"You speak well already!" exclaimed the father underneath his long beard.

Nora's sister, a twenty-something girl wearing a matching red sweatsuit, smacked her father on the arm and yelled something in Farsi.

"Oh, you study books?!?!" he said again, laughing at himself.

"Yes, exactly," replied Ava, smiling.

"So you going to help our Bobo get grades better?" asked Nora's mother, nodding her head over at Nora.

"Yes, I can help. We have a lot of work to do," Ava said, hinting that maybe she and Nora should go upstairs and get started on her homework.

"Very nice," smiled Nora's father. "Good dinner, Soha," he said to his wife. Soha smiled, her dimples emerging on her rosy cheeks.

Nora's brother didn't say much. He ate quickly and occasionally looked up to wink at Ava.

The family continued eating and engaged in pleasant conversation. All the while, Ava was confused that maybe they thought she was supposed to be here for two hours. Maybe they thought they would eat for one and then study for the second? Suddenly Ava looked down at her watch. She had been there one hour and 10 minutes. She was already late for Vanessa Taft's house.

She looked up at Nora's mother, and said, "Thank you so much. Dinner was so lovely, unfortunately I have another student right now."

"Oh, so sorry for keeping you!" Soha exclaimed, "Nora, show her out. So, next time, same time, yes? We are having lamb, ok?"

"Thank you, " Ava replied, "See you then."

Nora showed Ava back to the monstrous door and gave Ava a hug. "Bye," she said shyly as she looked down at the ground, "Thanks for coming."

Ava walked out the front door and back into her car. That was the easiest hour she had ever worked in her entire life. Were they going to do that every time? She would remind herself not to eat on the days she went there. It was absolutely delicious.

20

$\mathcal{A}$va pulled out of the Zhirhanian driveway and onto busy Benedict Canyon. She drove into the flats of Beverly Hills and pulled up to a large Mediterranean-style home. She noticed that the street was familiar and it dawned on her, "Oh, right up the street from Stan Smith. How convenient."

Ava parked on the street and walked up to the front door. The house was large, pink, and sat behind a front yard filled with tropical plants. It was beautiful and inviting, although it looked about 6,000 square feet. It was less intimidating that the other houses she worked at. No large gates, no security cameras. Ava didn't feel like an intruder here. Classical music crept out the window.

Ava rang the doorbell. The door opened seconds after. A perfect 16-year-old schoolgirl stood in front of her. Her hair was in two braids and she wore a traditional schoolgirl uniform; a plaid skirt and a loose white blouse. On her neck hung a gold crucifix. A true parent's dream come true.

"A pleasure to meet you, Miss Fleet. I'm Vanessa," said the perfect schoolgirl in flawless, polite, almost robotic speech as she offered a firm handshake. "Let me show you to the library. I have a great deal of studying to do today. Let's get started."

Ava couldn't believe her luck today. First, the Persian feast and now her very own schoolgirl Sandra Dee. Life couldn't get any easier. Vanessa led Ava to a magnificent library lined with classic books. On the huge mohagany desk sat Vanessa's homework, already opened to the proper page. Ava was in heaven. This was going to be a breeze.

Ava and Vanessa sat next to each other at the desk and began to work. "I've already done all of my assigned homework for the night, so I'd like to get started on studying for my literature midterm. It is in three weeks. Before I study, I like to pray. Will you join me?"

Ava was on autopilot. Vanessa was a dream come true. She wanted to study for a test three weeks away and pray before doing it. Unbelievable. Ava breezed through the hour and Vanessa even asked Ava to stay five extra minutes. Ava wondered why Vanessa's grades were so poor. She couldn't understand it.

"Thank you so much for coming. I must get ready for Polo practice now," Vanessa said in the sweetest voice to ever enter Ava's ears.

Ava left the house feeling like she had just struck gold. The Zhirhanian family and Vanessa were the most wonderful people she had ever met. To what did she owe this reward? Ava did not know what she had done to deserve such good fortune, but she was indeed thankful.

Ava drove home to her sorority house feeling the happiest she had ever felt in a long time. Her two hours of work today had gone smoothly and she actually looked forward to going back to tutor Nora Zhirhanian and Vanessa Taft. As she pulled into the driveway of Kappa Kappa Gamma, she decided she deserved some fun. When Bobbi inevitably asks her to go out tonight, Ava decided she was going to say yes. The day had been going so well, why not have little fun.

21

Ten o'clock rolled around as Ava tried on different outfits and played with her makeup. She had not gone out with her girlfriends in so long, she hardly knew what was appropriate to wear anymore.

Bobbi walked in the door of their room and dropped all her shopping bags and her jaw as she saw Ava getting ready to go out. "Um, am I hallucinating? Shouldn't you be, like, at the library?"

"No, tonight I am taking the night off," Ava announced.

Bobbi squealed and jumped up and down. "How perfect!!! I just got back from Neimen Marcus Last Call sale, where I met this producer guy and he invited me to go out with him to some hot place. The Whiskey I think. Oh my God, we're so going. We're so partying like rock stars! Ahhhh!!!"

An hour later, Ava and Bobbi Francis walked out the front door of Kappa Kappa Gamma. "OK, we're in front," Bobbi said into her cell phone. She snapped it shut and then told Ava, "He'll be here in five minutes."

Like clockwork, in five minutes, a beautiful red Ferrari pulled in front of Kappa Kappa Gamma. Ava and Bobbi walked toward the car and an all-too-familiar face got out of the driver's side.

"Hey babe," Stan Smith said with his big smile that said *Everyone wants me and I know it*!

"You know each other?" Bobbi asked, confused.

"Um, well, yeah, I-"Ava began.

"You know, I know everyone in LA, baby, I told you that at Neimen's," said Stan Smith to an ever-curious Bobbi.

Ava was stuck. She finally agreed to go out with Bobbi and who picks them up but Stan Smith. Oh well, there was no turning back. Anyway, Ava kind of liked and appreciated Stan Smith, now that he was not her employer. He was sexy, wealthy, and funny, and he didn't try to hide the fact that he used all those things to get as much ass as possible. He didn't make up any stories or pretend he was something he wasn't. He was an honest and up-front guy, and in Los Angeles that was certainly a trait to be applauded. He was funny and unique. He was starting to grow on her. She liked him and she liked the Gucci bag he gave her too.

Tonight she was going to have a good time. Wherever they were going, there were sure to be a lot of other people. Ava would just make conversation with someone else and then say she was tired early and take a cab home.

Stan Smith rubbed Bobbi's leg as the three of them drove away. Ava wanted to ask Stan Smith about Annabelle, but she didn't think it was appropriate. She really wanted to know how she was doing. She was probably at home alone with Olivia. Ava missed her friend.

Stan Smith, Bobbi, and Ava pulled up to a fancy hotel just south of the Sunset Strip. A valet took Stan Smith's Ferrari and the three of them walked up behind a crowd of thirty people trying to get past the velvet rope and into the hotel lobby. Stan Smith stuck up his hand and the doorman yelled, "Let these three through!" The crowd parted and they walked into the hopping hotel lobby.

As Ava looked around, she was reminded of the party with Angelica Thurman. This felt the same, but smaller and more exclusive. Stan held Bobbi's hand and led her and Ava through a crowd of beautiful people to a table with a bottle of Dom Perignon ready to go. The classic rock music was blasting. A stick-thin waitress wearing a black catsuit came over and poured each of them a glass of champagne.

Ava felt like a puppet sitting on this plush couch next to Stan Smith. She and Bobbi were merely accessories, but Bobbi didn't seem to mind, as Stan Smith kissed her on the cheek. A tall, tanned, loud man walked over and handed Stan Smith a cigar as he gave him a high five. "Where have you been, dude, I haven't seen you around?" asked Stan Smith.

"Just got back from the Bahamas, " the tall guy announced. "Smoke that puppy," he said, pointing to the cigar, "It is dark, dark, dark. Hey, who are these two hot mamas?"

"This is Ava and Brandi," Stan Smith said, as he lit up the cigar.

"Bobbi!" exclaimed Bobbi, playfully smacking him.

"Yeah, Bobbi," he said, obviously not caring.

"That one's pretty cute," the tall guy said, pointing at Ava.

Ava was glad he said something to her. Now she felt cool and comfortable in this place. She welcomed the opportunity to venture away from Bobbi and Stan Smith for a little while. She stood up quickly and shook his hand. "Nice to meet you," she said.

She walked over and stood next to him. "Now, you're a nice girl. What are you doing in this kind of place?" he asked as he showed her around the hotel lobby. It was packed with people who all seemed to know this guy.

"Dave!" "Hey!" slick guys yelled at him.

"Hey sexy! Hi baby!" girls squealed as they hugged him.

"Oh, by the way, I'm David," he said.

Ava smiled. He actually was pretty nice. He led her around, introducing her to people. David led her back to a small VIP room where it was very dark. Although it was hard to see, Ava could make out the faces of a few famous rock stars who snorted lines of cocaine with a bevy of beautiful women.

"Now, I'm not into this stuff, " David announced, pointing at the drug-laden table, "But if you are, go ahead."

"No thanks," Ava said.

David smiled back at her.

Ava watched the VIP table of rockers and models, all high out of their minds. Some of the girls looked like they were no more than sixteen years old. Ava was intrigued by the situation. What did these girls tell their parents when they left the house? Maybe they snuck out the window? Who knew?

Ava watched a particular girl who honestly looked to be fourteen years old. She sat on the lap of a famous rock-and-roll star who Ava knew had been arrested for beating his wife. The girl's long brown hair was draped over her shoulders. It stopped right below tiny breasts that formed into cleavage by a heavy duty push up bra and topped off with a skull and crossbones tattoo. The tattoo looked fake. She leaned over the table and snorted a huge line. As her head swung up and she wiped her nose with her wrist, her eyes met Ava's. Suddenly Ava remembered those eyes from earlier in the day. No, it couldn't be true. Ava looked at her again to be absolutely sure. When the little girl jumped off the rock star's lap and ran over to Ava and gave her a hug, Ava's worst fears were confirmed.

"Hi, Miss Fleet, its me, Vanessa, remember, from today?" she asked.

Ava was in shock. The perfect little angel from this afternoon was standing right there in a drug laden VIP room wearing a leather miniskirt, fishnet stockings, a very, very low cut top, dark makeup and a TATTOO!

David also gave Vanessa a hug. "Hey baby!" she

squealed. Unbelievable. Vanessa Taft, Ava's perfect homework angel, was a drug addict who had been doing this for years. Ava's heart dropped as Vanessa danced back over to her rock star boyfriend.

"Let's get out of here, huh?" David asked, nudging Ava.

"Yeah," Ava whispered. She was so shocked, she could barely speak.

David led Ava back to the main lobby, where even more Beautiful People cavorted. As the people became more drunk, the party became rowdier. Scantily clad girls danced on the tables. Even more people waited outside to get past the velvet rope; there must have been fifty by now. The music was louder and voices were raised to accommodate. Ava had read about the famous nightclub Studio 54. She imagined this is what it must have been like. She had never been to such a place in her entire life. She took in everything with awe as she walked around, still in shock after running into Vanessa Taft. What a sweet little girl she thought she was. Only hours after meeting her and deciding she was a dream come true did Ava find her in a dark room snorting drugs off a glass table. It seemed everything in this town was not what it seemed. Everything had a duplicitous nature that more often than not was disappointing.

David led Ava back to the table where Stan Smith and Bobbi had now finished the bottle of champagne and were making out.

"There's your cronies," David announced, pointing at them.

They didn't even look up.

"It's one o'clock, I'm getting out of here," David said.

Ava was tired. She wanted to go home too. "I'm going to get a cab in front," she said.

"I'll walk you out," David said politely.

Ava leaned over and told Bobbi she was going home. Bobbi just waved her hand and didn't seem to notice or care. Ava had not been missed in the hour or so she had been gone.

David led Bobbi toward the front. They walked past the crowd trying to get in as David said goodbye to the doorman. "See you next week," he said.

After Ava made it past the crowd of people and several paparazzi assembled outside, she dug in her handbag for her cell phone. "I wish I had the number of a cab programmed in here," she thought to herself. She hated having to call information. It cost $1.25 just to get a phone number that she could have looked up before she left! She dialed 411 as David handed the valet his ticket. As she got the number of the cab, suddenly Ava felt like doing something she usually did not ever have the guts to do. "Would you give me a ride home?" she asked David, barely able to believe her own mouth.

David smiled. "Sure, I wanted to ask you if you wanted one, but I thought you might misinterpret me. I didn't want to offend you."

His car pulled up. It was a beautiful silver Bentley Azure. Ava got inside as David handed the valet a crisp fifty-dollar bill, and didn't wait for the change.

"Thanks," she said.

"No problem," he replied, "Now where might you live?" he asked.

"Westwood, by UCLA," she replied.

"Oh, right on my way, you couldn't have picked a more convenient location to live," he joked.

What a gentleman. Ava could not believe that in the hotel lobby full of crazy people she actually met a tried-and-true gentleman.

He pulled up to Kappa Kappa Gamma. "Sweet dreams," he said, as the car rolled to a halt.

"Thanks for the ride," she replied, almost nervously.

She got out of the car and walked up the steps. She punched the code to the front door and opened it. She turned around and waved to him. He had waited to make sure she got in safely. Ava giggled inside. What could have been a horrible night ended up nicely.

22

*A*va tapped her pencil on the desk, debating between two answers. She had eliminated C, D, and A...only B or E was correct. She tapped her pencil back and forth on the answers. B, no E....E no B...Fuck it...Ava filled in B. She already had filled in so many Es on this test, the best guess was that there would not be another one. She walked up to the front of the classroom and handed Professor Simons her scantron. She was glad she was done. Multiple choice tests were difficult. At least on essay tests she could improvise and use her sophisticated vocabulary to dance around the answers. On a multiple choice, no chance. There was only one right answer and four wrong ones. No gray area to play with.

Professor Simons smiled at Ava. Her beady eyes were barely visible behind her thick spectacles and curly gray hair. Ava smiled back and walked out the back door of the classroom, wondering whether Professor Simons really was a woman.

Ava walked quickly to her car. She had to get to Little Z's house in 15 minutes.

23

$\mathcal{A}$fter another eventful and productive tutoring session with Little Z, Ava drove slowly out of Bel Air as her cell phone rang. She recognized the caller ID as the Kurakis house, and was surprised. She wasn't scheduled to come back for two days.

"Amy, there is an emergency." It was Angelica Thurman.

"You are calling Ava, the tutor, right?" Ava replied.

"Whatever - We are going to our villa in Portofino tomorrow and you need to come with us. Jarrod, Carson, and I are throwing a little party for my dear friend Giorgio Armani. We need you to come with us, dear. Carson absolutely must not fall behind in addition or whatever. So, we will see you tomorrow at 4:00. Van Nuys airport. Thanks, bye."

"Uh - bye." Ava could barely catch her breath before she could agree or disagree. But with Angelica Thurman, disagreement was not an option. Two days was officially the start of spring break where Ava was all set up to go to Evan Shapiro's time-share in Cabo. Now, her plans were suddenly steam-rolled by Angelica Thurman. But not really though. Italy. Beautiful scenery and beaches. Jarrod. OK, maybe spring break was going to be better than originally planned.

The next day, Ava pulled up to Van Nuys airport. She had never been there before. Why was it so small? She walked to the number four hangar where Jonathan had told her to meet them when he called earlier. There, getting out of the Kurakis family limo were Angelica, Carson, and Jarrod. Carson and Jarrod were in matching suits with the Kurakis family emblem on them. Carson looked adorable, like a little angel. Jarrod looked like a dream come true. As the three Kurakis's, Ava, and Jonathan boarded the Kurakis family jet, Ava held her breath. She had never been on a private plane before and, wow, was it amazing. It had beautiful, plush, white, leather couches and wood trim. Everything about it was clean and flawless. Ava walked in and took a seat next to Jarrod. The flight was long but enjoyable. Angelica mostly slept in the large chair. She wore a black sleeping mask that read "pussycat" spelled out in pink Swarovski crystals. Angelica had an interesting sleep-talking habit. She would suddenly dart up out of her chair, command Jonathan to spray her face with her Evian facial mister or bark random orders at non-present people; "Get me these Jimmy Choos in a size five!" and "Victor, we're out of Dom!"

Carson asked Ava to read several books to her, and at one time Jarrod fell asleep and rested on Ava's shoulder while she read to Carson.

As they began the descent into the Genoa airport, Ava watched out the window excitedly. The city looked so magical and beautiful. Carson kept telling Ava how happy

143

he was that she was with them and how he didn't want to go to the boring party.

The Kurakis villa in Portofino was amazing. The tall Mediterranean structure towered over the flat land around it. Fountains and beautiful gardens covered the grounds.

Jonathan led Ava to her room. It was evening now, and everyone was going right to bed. After Ava put on her pajamas, she stood by the French doors looking out over the ocean as it twinkled in the night. It looked magical. Ava stood for at least twenty minutes just gazing at the view. She could imagine nothing more fantastic.

She turned around to find Jarrod Kurakis standing right in front of her. He took her hand. What had gone unsaid for so long could finally be spoken, but not in words. He looked deeply into her eyes as he ran his fingers through her hair. He caressed her cheek. Her heart beat quickly as he held her hand and then ran his fingers up her back. His mouth molded into hers as he kissed her with the love of a man well beyond his years. The few men before him didn't matter anymore. What she felt for him was layered and complicated and very wrong. He kissed her softly on each cheek and on her eye and then her mouth again. He held her close to him and rubbed his hands all over her body. Ava was amazed at how much he knew. The way his body moved, she could not believe he was only seventeen. The magnificent Italian moonlight reflected off their hot skin as what had been only imagined by both parties immediately become a reality. The ramifications could not be handled by either, but that didn't matter now. In fact, nothing mattered now, as they both did what they had thought about for so long.

All that mattered was Ava and Jarrod and the Italian night, which belonged to them, and them alone.

The next morning Ava awoke, wondering if the night before had been a dream. The handwritten note next to her bed confirmed it to be true.

"You are more beautiful than I imagined and it was better than I could have even thought. See you at breakfast. Love, J"

Ava showered, dressed and walked downstairs where a large Italian woman was cooking bacon, eggs, and toast for the whole Kurakis family. Ava ate slowly and in silence with the rest of the Kurakis family. Ava looked over at Angelica several times scared to death that this woman might know about her son's adventure last night. What had happened was so out of character for Ava Fleet. At home, it was illegal - but was it really wrong? Thank God it had happened in Europe.

Jarrod snuck winks and smiles at Ava and whispered to her to not be so scared of his mom, she was really a nice lady. The rest of the trip went smoothly. Ava mostly spent time coloring with Carson and doing addition. One night when she got in bed, she found a small velvet box underneath her pillow. Inside was a beautiful heart shaped diamond necklace from Jarrod. She put it on, slept in it, and didn't take it off for the rest of the trip. When Angelica had the party for Giorgio Armani, Ava sat with Carson in his room and played card games. Despite all the beautiful and famous people downstairs, all Ava could think about was Jarrod.

When they flew home, Ava was actually disappointed that the trip was over. It was her first time in Italy and it had been a quick trip for only three days. She decided for her next visit that she definitely needed more time. It had been fun, and when she added up all the hours she had been there and Angelica handed her a check, $10.00 per hour didn't seem so small anymore.

24

$\mathcal{A}$va pulled up to kiosk number one at the Kurakis house, where to her surprise, she was stopped. She thought she was a regular now. What was this all about?

"Why are you here?" the security guard asked.

"I am always here at this time," Ava said.

"Well, they're not here. I think they are in Malibu. Now run along, have a nice day."

Ava made a U-turn, a little confused as to where to go. Ava called the Kurakis house. No answer. Ava sat in her parked car at the bottom of the driveway. Then, Ava did the unthinkable. She took out Angelica Thurman's cell phone number which Ava was to call only in an extreme emergency.

"Who's this?" Angelica's voice snapped on the other end.

"Oh, hi this is Ava, the tutor-

147

"Where are you?!?! Anastasia-we have been waiting for fifteen minutes! Where are you? I am disappointed. I expect you to be here on time. The boys do not do well when their schedule is disrupted. And why are you calling me here anyway? Call the house-

"I did, but.."

"Oh, nevermind, come to Malibu, we're in Malibu." With that, Angelica Thurman hung up and Ava was left wondering exactly where in Malibu they were. Malibu was a big place; twenty-seven miles of scenic beauty according to the "Welcome to Malibu" sign. In exactly what part of the twenty-seven miles could the Kurakis family be? Ava decided that she had already done the unthinkable once, why not do it twice.

"Why are you calling again? I expect you to be here."

"I'm very sorry Ms. Thurman, but I don't know where in Malibu you are."

"Oh...my...God...Hello? We're at my house."

"Yes, but Ms. Thurman, what is the address? I've never been there."

"Oh, please. Jonathan, what is the address here? I can't deal with this moron."

"Hi, Ava, its me, Jonathan. Yes we are at 535 Pacific Coast Highway. Now, please hurry up, we've been waiting and you're late."

Ava hung up the phone feeling very frustrated. As she drove towards Malibu she couldn't help but feel sad about the way Angelica treated her. She felt she had been tricked. Furthermore, why was she so mad at her for being late? Was she supposed to have a LoJack on the Kurakis family and be able to find them at all times? No one had told her to go to Malibu. She had gone to their spread in Bel Air as always. She just didn't get it sometimes.

Jarrod looked up and smiled when he saw Ava enter the room. His face was slightly red with embarrassment. Hunky Jarrod, star of the football team and high school hottie, sat cross legged on the floor reading to his younger brother. Ava thought it was the most adorable thing she had ever seen. Jarrod, on the other hand, would have personally killed Ava had she ever told anyone that. He was not cute, he had a tough image to uphold, and sitting on the floor reading a fairy tale did not contribute positively to an image of a hard-to-get stud. Jarrod got up and decided he urgently needed to go to the weight room and bench press upwards of 240 pounds.

As he walked by Ava, his bare arm brushed up against hers, and she got goosebumps as he pinched her butt. "See you in an hour, teach," he said coolly as he walked away.

Carson jumped up and hugged Ava excitedly.

"I was waiting sooo long for you, tutor. I was sad and I thought you weren't coming. "

"No worries, Carson, let's get going," she said.

Carson's room was a duplicate of his room in Bel Air, with a beachside theme. He still had the life-size FAO

Schwartz animals, but they were turtles, fish, and stuffed palm trees instead. On his bed sat an island-themed comforter, and about two-hundred puffy pillows with palm trees on them. There were also the Tiffany silver picture frames with photos of many tanned beautiful people wearing white. There was a picture of Carson, Angelica, Pamela Anderson and her two children playing in the ocean. A photo of Carson and Jarrod sitting on a rock caught Ava's eye. Jarrod looked like a Tommy Hilfiger model sitting on the rock, dressed in a crisp white shirt. His tan and blonde highlights looked amazing in the sunlight. He was perfect.

"We have lots of coloring today, tutor," Carson began as he opened a drawer to reveal a brand new set of markers in a hundred colors. Ava sat with Carson as they sat at his desk and colored a large placemat by number. Color it red if it begins with the number one, color is blue if it ends in zero, and make your own number pattern with the color green. Carson concentrated as if each number was an SAT question, reminding Ava of Jarrod's upcoming SAT. She was having so much fun hanging out with Jarrod, she had nearly forgotten that he was going to take the SAT exam soon. She really had to work hard with him these next few weeks or he would not score high enough. Coloring with Carson was so much fun. Why couldn't she just do this all day long? The hour was up.

"Excellent coloring Carson, you're the next Warhol," Ava said.

"Huh?" he said, confused, and then smiled, "Go see my brother now, I am going in the jacuzzi with mommy," as he jumped up, ran down the hall, and called for his mother.

Ava left Carson and walked to Jarrod's room. She

found him crouched over his desk, his head in his hands. He didn't even look up when she walked in. She walked over, pulled up a chair next to him, and sat down.

"What's up," she asked.

Jarrod turned his head towards her and looked in her eyes with a look of pure terror. "This is the scariest thing I have ever seen," he replied, as he held up his "How to Prepare for the SAT" book.

"I have read the same paragraph over and over and I still don't understand what it says. I have never felt so dumb in my life. I can't believe there is actually something I have no way out of. My whole life, I have been able to pay or charm my way out of everything. I am being completely honest with you, Ava, there is no way out of this one, even with my special circumstances."

"What do you mean? What special circumstances?" Ava asked. She was genuinely concerned about him. She didn't just think he was cute anymore. This was no longer just a physical attraction or a crush. Ava truly cared about this family. She had been working with them almost a year now, and had grown to love each one of them, as bizarre as they were. She didn't feel like a coach anymore; she felt like a fan. She wanted so much for them to all do well in life and overcome their respective obstacles.

"Because of my ADD. I get to take the test alone with an official proctor. That part is no problem. My mom will just pay for Jonathan to be trained as an official proctor. But, the whole test has to be videotaped by someone the ETS sends themselves and it has to be an approved testing location. I have to take the test myself. There is no way out of it. I need at least a 1200 to get into Oxford. My dad and all his six brothers went there. It is a Kurakis family legacy. I have to get in. Even with my family legacy, I still need an acceptable score or they won't let me in. Most people who get in there get a 1400 or above."

"Jarrod, you can do it. You can do well on this test. We will work hard," Ava began, reassuring him.

Just then, Angelica Thurman walked in wearing a shimmery gold bikini and matching heels. She ran over to Jarrod and gave him a big bear hug. Ava could smell the alcohol on Angelica's breath.

"What is my baby gonna do?" she whined. "SAT is no fun and too hard. Mommy never took it...I wish baby didn't have to do it."

Jarrod rolled his eyes. "Yeah mom, whatever. I don't think you were interested in the same major I am."

"Major? Ha ha ha, I was already on the cover of *Elle* at your age," squealed Angelica, as she posed like a model.

Jarrod rolled his eyes again. "Exactly."

Just then Angelica's eyes lit up as she squealed, "EEEE, mommy has a good idea. I want to take the pressure off my baby," she said.

She ran over and closed the door, as if she, Ava, and

Jarrod were in a top-secret meeting. She hunched over Ava and Jarrod and whispered, "OK, so here's what we will do. Baby and Anastasia will go together to the normal group test, not the special ADD one."

"That would be you," Jarrod said as he looked at Ava and smiled.

Angelica continued, "Yes, you, heeee heee...OK, so you two will both register for the test. You will go to the test together and Baby will write tutor's name on his test and tutor will write Baby's name on her test and voila! Baby gets a good score and tutor gets a bad score but who cares because my baby will be in college like Mommy is at Neiman Marcus!"

Ava and Jarrod stared at each other with blank faces. Angelica stared back at them with radiant 500-watt eyeballs and two thousand shiny pearly teeth. She was beyond pleased with her problem-solving skills. Jarrod was happy too, but stared at Ava to see her reaction.

Ava looked back at them and knew the plan would work. It was foolproof. Ava could register for the test as a regular test taker. She could check in at the door and show her ID. That was the only checkpoint as she remembered it three years ago when she took the SAT. She would walk in, take the test, and write Jarrod Kurakis' name on it. Then she would hand it in. As she walked out the door, they would check her ID again. As she remembered, they never actually checked to see if the name on the test matched the name on the ID. They only checked to see if the person was a registered tester. It was flawless. It would work perfect- ly. Ava wanted nothing more than to help Jarrod. She liked him and had grown to care about him and his family.

"I can't do it," Ava said, as she looked down at the floor.

"Please," pleaded Jarrod.

"Name your price. Whatever you want. Whatever it takes," said Angelica.

"I just can't," Ava said. She could not look up from the floor. She wanted so badly to help, but taking the SAT for Jarrod just wasn't right. If she were caught, it would mean so many bad things...

"One million - cash," said Angelica.

"Mom!" Jarrod shouted, shocked.

"Ava (Ava was shocked-her real name!) this is very important to our family. You will not get caught. We know people in VERY high places. I have never met a cop I couldn't pay off. You have nothing to worry about." Angelica explained, as Jarrod leaned in closer and looked at Ava and winked. She was being let in on a special family secret. They were trusting her with information that was very sacred.

"Look at all this around you, Ava? Wealth doesn't just buy you jewelry and fancy clothes. That is not really what money is for. My husband wasn't satisfied with controlling and running legitimate businesses. He doesn't just own things, he owns people. He had three families backing him, and that means they're behind me, his sons, and now...you."

Ava was shocked and she couldn't do anything but look at the floor and then into Angelica's serious face. Ava had never seen her look so serious, even though Angelica was wearing the shiny gold bikini. No wonder there were

154

always men in black suits following Angelica; she had more security than most movie stars, and that was because Angelica Thurman was not just a movie star, she was something else altogether.

Angelica put her hand on Ava's back. "You think about it, baby." Angelica said.

Ava said goodbye to Jarrod and walked slowly out of the room with Angelica. They walked down the hallway, and stopped for a moment at Angelica's room. Angelica told Ava to wait for a minute as she walked in, and emerged holding a small silk bag. She grabbed Ava's hand again and led her to the front door. She handed her the silk bag and looked at her seriously and deeply into both eyes.

"You think about it," she said, " This college system is so stiff. It puts too much pressure on my boy to get in. If you help us out, you will be set for life."

Ava started to speak but Angelica cut her off. She pointed at the silk bag and said slowly again, "Think about it."

Ava walked out the front door of the Kurakis beachfront paradise and into the dark evening. As she drove away, she looked up to see Carson, Jarrod, and Angelica watching her from the window. Their dark silhouettes looked like large stone statues as they watched her drive away into the Malibu night.

When Ava had reached the bottom of the driveway, and was back on PCH, she stopped at the first stop sign. There was not a soul in sight. Ava loosened the strings on the silk bag Angelica had given her. She felt around inside and then took a look. She counted each one hundred dollar bill slowly. Then she counted once again to be sure. Ten thousand dollars cash - nice advance.

25

The next two weeks went by slowly and were filled with apprehension. Right after Ava and Jarrod took the SAT together, the Kurakis family left on their private jet to Greece to tend to some official business. Ava's tenure at the Kurakis house had ended. The last day with them had been one filled with tension. They didn't like Ava's moral approach to life, but they admired her diligence in preparing Jarrod for the SAT.

After Angelica and Jarrod's proposition in Malibu, Ava went back and forth in her mind over what to do. She wanted to say yes more than anything. She thought about it night and day. She wrote lists of the pros and cons, and the pros looked very tempting. She did not sleep for days. All she could think about was the SAT. She could not pay attention in class. She stared out the window, looking for a big red arrow pointing the way. She wanted to do it so badly, but she knew deep down it was not honest. Finally, she made a decision.

Ava made a proposition of her own. She explained to Angelica that students could take the SAT several times. Ava suggested that she tutor Jarrod for the few weeks prior to the SAT. She would devote all her free time to his SAT studying, and she had truly kept her promise. The last few weeks before the exam, Ava had practically lived at the Kurakis house. She sometimes stayed until 3:00 am going over and over SAT questions with Jarrod. She had literally given every free minute to helping him study for the SAT.

She told Angelica to just pay the normal hourly rate. All the hours of studying would earn Ava more money than she had ever expected anyway. Helping Jarrod was her job. She cared about doing a good job. She cared about him and the rest of the Kurakis family. Angelica laughed hysterically at Ava's plan, insisted she was crazy, and assured Ava she was wasting her time. She found the plan so outlandish, in fact, that she even promised that, if it worked, she would be more than willing to throw in "a little something extra."

Ava went with Jarrod to the SAT, but just for moral support. She put her own name on her own test, and he put his name on his test. She wanted to see if he could get the score on his own, after all the hours of studying. If he didn't get it, he could always take it again, and maybe they would do it Angelica's way, but Ava pleaded with them to please try it her way, just once, just for the first time. Ava hoped it would work. Deep down, she wanted to see Jarrod do it himself.

The last time Ava saw the Kurakis family together was when Angelica and Carson pulled up in the family limousine, driven by Victor. Ava waved at them and Angelica looked at her with a shrug of the shoulders that said, "We'll see..."

After taking the SAT, Ava thought about the recent events. So much had occurred since she last took the SAT, in high school. She had completed three years of college already, of which she was proud. She was also nervously thinking about the future and what she would do with her life. However, she was proud of what she had done so far.

Little Z was ready for his world rap tour. He had even invited Ava to see his show at the Staples Center in a few months and told her she could, "hang backstage with him and the rest of the honeys."

Vanessa Taft was off to a boarding school, which was probably a better situation for her. Maybe she would find more direction. At least she was willing to go, with Ava's convincing - it was better than being forced by her parents. Nora Zhirhanian had received all A's in her advanced placement courses and had an internship at the White House for the summer. She was quite an accomplished girl, especially for only being in high school. She would go far in life, but would always come home. How could she resist the fantastic home cooked meals from her mother?

Then there was Ava's precious Annabelle. She was a smart little girl and Ava only hoped that she would grow up to be as beautiful an adult as she was a child. Ava always felt a deep sadness when she thought about how the Smith family had let her go, though she knew it was for the best. It had been too much to handle. Ava had become too involved and placed in too many compromising situations. She had come to terms with the dismissal. There was only so much she could do.

The Kurakis family dominated Ava's thoughts. She had become so involved with a family that she had barely known eight months ago. So many emotions were felt for this family. They existed as a phenomenon in her life she never knew existed. How could she love one person, care about another as her own child, and have a bizarre indefinable friendship with their mother? It was unexplainable and bizarre. Ava felt attachments she had never felt before and probably never would again.

Ava passed the next few weeks taking her finals and packing up her room to move home for the summer. She found a job at a video game company near where her parents lived. She was going to help test new video games with groups of elementary school children. She could live at her parents' house and be with her family. She was happy about it. She would be going home soon.

Ava spent more time with her friends. She went to barbeques at Evan's house. She had dinners with David.

One night David took her to the trendy Ivy and sometimes they just barbequed at his house. She loved Jarrod, but David was a man. He was older, more established, and set in his ways. Jarrod was young, exciting, and had no potential. He sent her nice love letters, but none of them ever mentioned the SAT. Ava was excited to see him when he got back. He even invited her to have dinner with him on his eighteenth birthday that summer. Both David and Jarrod filled certain voids in Ava's life. First and foremost, Ava Fleet was a career girl. She wanted to create her own identity before becoming a part of someone else's. However, what went unspoken between David and Ava was understood by both of them. David was older and liked his life as a cool bachelor. He wasn't quite ready to give that up yet. Ava didn't make any decisions about the future. She just treated the relationship lightly. They had fun together and that was that. They were good friends who flirted here and there.

Ava often walked in the park or went to the beach to rollerblade. She checked her messages every three hours, hoping to hear from the Kurakis family. She was dying to know what happened with the SAT score, but she tried to occupy herself with other things so that she would not drive herself crazy waiting to hear. Ava even did a little shopping. She went to Fred Segal one day, where she ran into Vanessa Taft and her mom. Vanessa had dyed her hair pink and was wearing torn jeans. Mrs. Taft stood next to her in a cashmere sweater and Ferragamo ballet slippers and seemed to be proud of her daughter's individuality. They asked Ava to join them for lunch. Ava had an iced tea and then went home.

One morning, Ava sat downstairs in the dining room of Kappa Kappa Gamma reading the paper by herself, as usual. Three and a half weeks had passed since the SAT and she could not believe she had not yet heard from the Kurakis family. Bobbi skipped down the stairs in a matching pink tracksuit and rhinestone sunglasses.

159

"Oh my God, do you want to go to the Red Hot Chili Peppers concert tonight??? I have an extra ticket. It's two hundred bucks, but they are REALLY good seats!"

Normally Ava would never spend so much on a concert, but it was the end of the school year and Ava had worked hard. Ava had used all her bonuses from Little Z and the Kurakis family to pay off her tuition. Their tips combined with her scholarship meant she never would have to worry about tuition or books again. Ava thought about going to the concert with Bobbi. Maybe she would go, if it worked out in her budget.

"Can I get back to you in like a half hour?"

"EEEEE! Sure, let me know!" Bobbi squealed, as she ran into the living room to watch *Sex and the City*.

Ava thought it might be fun. She had to verify her checking account balance first though. She wanted to be sure she would still be comfortable for the month.

Ava walked upstairs and dialed the 1-800 number for her bank.

"Please enter your account number," the monotone computerized voice said.

Ava entered the seven-digit number and pressed #.

"For account balance press one."

Ava pressed one and sat down on her bed and fiddled with her hair.

Ava nearly fell off her bed and dropped the phone when she heard what the voice said.

"Your account balance is one million three hundred thirty two dollars and seventy three cents."

She went to the concert and had the time of her life.